REA

ALLEN COUNTY

P9-EDI-336

3 1833 05561 7689

"Sometimes I feel like I don't know what I'm doing."

Keri recognized her mistake almost as soon as the words left her mouth. "I shouldn't have said that. Especially to you."

"Why especially to me?" Grady leaned closer to her. He smelled clean and masculine.

"You'll think I don't know how to handle Bryan. But that's not true. He never gives me any trouble. He's a very good kid. I wish I could make you see that."

Grady's eyes didn't leave her face. "I see a woman two kids are very lucky to have in their lives," he said softly, touching her cheek.

The interior of the car created a cocoon containing just the two of them, their warm breath already starting to fog the windows. The air was a heady smell of warm skin and man. He moved imperceptibly toward her. He was going to kiss her. And she was going to let him.

ROMANCE

MAY 2 9 2008

Dear Reader,

How can a book that takes place in the world of high school basketball not be about sports? I hope *Anything for Her Children* answers that question.

Yes, the hero's a basketball coach. And yes, the heroine's son is the team's star player. But what happens off the court is so much more important and character defining than any of the games athletes play.

Anything for Her Children is about honor and integrity and doing the right thing. Those are the invaluable qualities that can be imparted through sports, qualities I hope both of my basketball-playing children are developing.

But most of all, the book is about love. Because, in the end, nothing is more important.

All my best,

Darlene Gardner

MAY 3 3 2008

ANYTHING FOR HER CHILDREN
Darlene Gardner

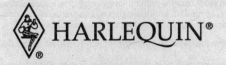

HARLEQUIN®

TORONTO • NEW YORK • LONDON
AMSTERDAM • PARIS • SYDNEY • HAMBURG
STOCKHOLM • ATHENS • TOKYO • MILAN • MADRID
PRAGUE • WARSAW • BUDAPEST • AUCKLAND

If you purchased this book without a cover you should be aware that this book is stolen property. It was reported as "unsold and destroyed" to the publisher, and neither the author nor the publisher has received any payment for this "stripped book."

ISBN-13: 978-0-373-71490-2
ISBN-10:   0-373-71490-4

ANYTHING FOR HER CHILDREN

Copyright © 2008 by Darlene Hrobak Gardner.

All rights reserved. Except for use in any review, the reproduction or utilization of this work in whole or in part in any form by any electronic, mechanical or other means, now known or hereafter invented, including xerography, photocopying and recording, or in any information storage or retrieval system, is forbidden without the written permission of the publisher, Harlequin Enterprises Limited, 225 Duncan Mill Road, Don Mills, Ontario, Canada M3B 3K9.

This is a work of fiction. Names, characters, places and incidents are either the product of the author's imagination or are used fictitiously, and any resemblance to actual persons, living or dead, business establishments, events or locales is entirely coincidental.

This edition published by arrangement with Harlequin Books S.A.

® and TM are trademarks of the publisher. Trademarks indicated with ® are registered in the United States Patent and Trademark Office, the Canadian Trade Marks Office and in other countries.

www.eHarlequin.com

Printed in U.S.A.

ABOUT THE AUTHOR

While working as a newspaper sportswriter, Darlene Gardner realized she'd rather make up quotes than rely on an athlete to say something interesting. So she quit her job and concentrated on a fiction career that landed her at Harlequin/Silhouette Books, where she's written for Harlequin Temptation, Harlequin Duets and Silhouette Intimate Moments before finding a home at Harlequin Superromance.

Please visit Darlene on the Web at www.darlenegardner.com.

Books by Darlene Gardner

HARLEQUIN SUPERROMANCE

1316–MILLION TO ONE
1360–A TIME TO FORGIVE
1396–A TIME TO COME HOME
1431–THE OTHER WOMAN'S SON

Don't miss any of our special offers. Write to us at the following address for information on our newest releases.

Harlequin Reader Service
U.S.: 3010 Walden Ave., P.O. Box 1325, Buffalo, NY 14269
Canadian: P.O. Box 609, Fort Erie, Ont. L2A 5X3

To my teenage son Brian for his invaluable input on the basketball scenes—and his suggestion that I name the heroine's son Bryan. Also, because I love him even more than he loves basketball.

CHAPTER ONE

IF THE FANS PACKING the Springhill High gymnasium had known about the Carolina State College scandal, they might have given Grady Quinlan an even icier reception.

They greeted the basketball players who ran single file onto the court with raucous cheers worthy of an undefeated team, but the ovation abruptly quieted to a murmur when Grady walked onto the hardwood.

Grady kept his expression carefully blank, a triumph considering he'd already weathered the resignation of his assistant coach earlier that evening.

"You got nothin' on Fuzz," Dan Cahill had said, referring to the longtime Springhill coach who'd suffered a heart attack over the Christmas holiday. "I can't work with someone I don't respect."

Grady had only taken over the job as the Springhill Cougars' head coach two weeks ago, but the crowd about to witness his debut didn't think much of him, either.

All because word had spread that Grady had suspended Bryan Charleton, the best player to come through Springhill High in a decade.

Grady looked over his shoulder, expecting to see Bryan bringing up the rear. The seventeen-year-old junior had shown up for the pregame talk wearing khaki pants and a dress shirt, demonstrating he knew the drill. A suspended player couldn't suit up but was expected to support his teammates from the bench.

"You know where Bryan is?" Grady asked the short, skinny ninth-grade boy acting as the team's manager.

The boy's eyes darted away from Grady's. "No," he said, then went back to filling a tray of paper cups with water.

Rap music from the school's PA system blared. Grady's head pounded and beads of sweat formed on his forehead. He fiddled with the tie he wore with one of the suits he'd bought after being named an assistant coach at Carolina State. The tie felt like a noose.

On court the Springhill players and their opponents went through layup and shooting drills. The illuminated numbers on the overhead scoreboard clock counted down the minutes remaining in the allotted warm-up period.

Nineteen. Eighteen. Seventeen.

And still no Bryan.

"I'll be right back," Grady told Sid Humphries, the very young junior-varsity coach he'd asked to act as his bench assistant during the game. "Have them do passing drills next."

Ignoring the panicked look in Sid's eyes, Grady hurried back in the direction of the locker room, the heels of his dress shoes clicking on the wood floor.

"Grady. Wait up." Tony Marco, the school's athletic director, caught up to him in the corridor that led from the gym to the rest of the building.

Nearly a half foot shorter than Grady's six-four, Tony

had a stockier build, a mustache and the dark coloring he'd inherited from his Italian father.

Nobody ever guessed Grady's mother and Tony's mother were sisters.

"Is it true you suspended Bryan Charleton?" Tony sounded as though he'd be more likely to believe aliens had invaded the White House.

"Yeah, it's true." Grady fought against taking offense at his cousin's tone. If not for Tony, Grady would still be driving an eighteen-wheeler instead of coaching basketball and teaching high school students. "I caught him cheating."

"Cheating?" Tony's thick black eyebrows rose toward his hairline. "In PE?"

"Not in PE. I teach a nutrition and exercise class, too."

"Isn't that an elective?"

"Doesn't matter," Grady said tightly. "Cheating's cheating."

"But…" Tony's voice trailed off, though not before Grady guessed he was thinking about the regrettable circumstances that had led Grady to Springhill High.

"Suspending Bryan Charleton wasn't smart," Tony said in a hushed tone.

Grady straightened his spine. "I don't agree."

"Listen, R.G." Tony placed a hand on his shoulder and used the nickname nobody but family called him. Grady's full name was Robert Grady Quinlan. "Next time something like this comes up, run it by me before you do anything."

Grady had to unclench his jaw to respond. "You asked me to coach this team, remember? You said I was the best man for the job."

Tony had approached Grady in a panic after Fuzz Cart-wright, who'd coached at Springhill for more than two decades, collapsed during a holiday tournament game. Tony claimed Dan Cahill, the first-year assistant, didn't have enough experience to lead the team. Grady initially refused, telling Tony he couldn't support himself on a high school coach's stipend. Tony's second offer included a teaching job at Springhill High taking over Cartwright's health and PE classes.

Sick of driving a truck and missing coaching so much it was almost a physical ache, Grady relented and moved to western Pennsylvania. But now he remembered the real reason he'd been reluctant to return to coaching: the ripple effects of the scandal. Even his cousin was second-guessing him.

"You *are* the best man to coach this team," Tony said.

"Then let me do my job." Grady moved away, his cousin's hand dropping from his shoulder, the sensation of isolation even more acute as he continued to the locker room.

Silence and the smell of dried sweat greeted him, fol-lowed by the clank of a metal locker closing. Grady turned a corner around a bank of lockers and spotted Bryan Charleton with one foot on a bench, lacing up his size fifteen Nike basketball shoes. He was already dressed in the black-and-gold Springhill colors, the snarling Couga on the left leg of his shorts seeming to mock Grady.

"What are you doing in uniform?" Grady asked.

Bryan had strong regular features, close-cropped brow hair and dark, soulful eyes that gave off the impression would take a lot to rattle him. "Getting ready for th game."

"You're suspended. You're not playing in the game."

Bryan straightened to his full height. Six foot five with a lean, muscular build and the wingspan of a pterodactyl, the boy had been born to play basketball.

"Aw, Coach, you don't really mean that," the kid said in his soft, unhurried voice. "We're playing a tough team. Everybody knows I've got to play if we're gonna win."

Grady couldn't dispute that. It was still early in his junior year, and Bryan was already attracting interest from college coaches, making it likely that scholarship offers were on the horizon. The undisputed star of the team, Bryan had already led Springhill to an 11-0 record. Many believed he was good enough to propel the team to a state championship.

"I don't say things I don't mean, Bryan."

"But, Coach, why have me sit out the game? You made your point. I learned my lesson."

It would have been so easy for Grady to give in. To his cousin Tony. To the Springhill fans who clamored to see the team's star on the court. To the players who wanted to win. And to Bryan, whose passion for the game had never been in question.

But giving in wouldn't help Bryan, who needed above all to learn there were consequences for his actions. It would be like handing the boy a free pass to do whatever he pleased, no matter how wrong.

"Change out of that uniform and go home, Bryan," Grady ordered. "I don't even want you on the bench to-night."

"What? You're not serious."

"I'm dead serious." Grady looked directly into the boy's

shock-filled eyes, hardening his resolve so he wasn't tempted to change his mind. "Here's another lesson you can learn. Defy me again and you're off the team."

Grady didn't wait for Bryan's reaction. He walked out of the locker room and into the fray, questioning why he'd let his love of the game prevail over his common sense, propelling him to take this coaching job. Because once again the atmosphere in the stuffy gym was as chilly as the January night.

It was going to be, he thought, a very long basketball season.

KERI CASSIDY RUSHED TO the foot of the stairs in the cramped ranch house she shared with her two teenagers, wishing she didn't feel as though she'd never catch up.

She was always hurrying. To her job in the advertising department of the town's newspaper. To the grocery store. The bank. The high school. The gym. The doctor's office.

Today was no exception. She and Rose barely had time to eat the egg rolls and shrimp fried rice she'd picked up on the way home before it was time to get ready for Bryan's basketball game.

She wondered if other single mothers couldn't quite get all aspects of their lives running smoothly or if her age and relative inexperience put her at a distinct disadvantage. At twenty-five, she felt more like a kid herself than a mother.

She cupped her hands over her mouth and called, "Rosie, hurry up or we'll be late for your brother's game."

"But I can't find my black boot," Rose yelled back. The distress weighing down the fourteen-year-old's syllables sounded as real as if she'd lost something really important. Like her homework.

"Wear your brown shoes, then," Keri shouted.

"I can't wear brown with black," Rose exclaimed, sounding horrified.

Keri ran lightly up the stairs and down the narrow hall. She longed to believe it was a healthy sign that Rose strived to look good.

Keri rounded the corner to Rose's bedroom. Clothes, books and piles of paper littered every surface, as though a strong wind had swept through the room, which was pretty much the way Rose's room always looked.

Rose stood at her closet door, wearing a black top, chunky necklace and belted, low-waisted blue jeans on her tall, thin body. Her long golden-brown hair was brushed to a shine and streamed down her back. She'd obviously taken pains with her appearance, but her shoulders were slightly hunched, her body language giving away her lack of confidence. The same as always.

The girl glanced at Keri, her large brown eyes mirroring her distress. "I don't know where it is."

Rose knelt somewhat awkwardly in front of her closet and haphazardly rummaged through it, her jeans drawing up to reveal the difference between her two legs.

The left one was covered with smooth plastic instead of skin.

"Did you try under the bed?" Keri asked.

Rose got to her feet, moved to the bed, then carefully lowered herself before continuing the search. The prosthesis slowed her down even though it had been three years since a car accident had claimed her leg—and her mother.

Keri swallowed the sadness that always rose inside her when she thought of Maddy Charleton.

She could still picture the way Maddy had looked in the break room at the *Springhill Gazette* on Keri's first day of work nearly four years ago. A shocking head of dyed red hair. A voice a few decibels too loud. An infectious laugh.

"What are you waiting for, girl?" Maddy had demanded from her seat amid a group of their advertising department coworkers. "Get some caffeine and get your butt over here."

Their friendship had blossomed from there. It didn't matter that Maddy was nearly fifteen years Keri's senior. With her blunt manner and outrageous sense of humor, Maddy breathed life into every gathering.

So much had changed, Keri thought. Maddy was gone, the victim of a patch of ice that had sent her compact car sliding into a tree. Keri had adopted her two children. And the original reason for Keri's move to western Pennsylvania had married someone else.

"You were right. It was under the bed." Rose held up a black leather boot with a two-inch heel, her young, unlined face lit by one of her too-rare smiles.

"Then put it on, girl, and let's go before we miss the entire first quarter. You know Bryan likes to see us in the stands."

Rose sat down on the bed and yanked on the half boot over her prosthetic foot, which she'd covered with a black sock dotted with gray stars.

"I don't know what your rush is," Rose said. "Bryan's not even playing tonight."

"Of course he's playing," Keri refuted. Chances were a couple of college recruiters would be in the stands to watch him. "Why would you say that?"

"I heard at school that new coach suspended him." Rose, two and a half years younger than her brother, was a freshman at Springhill High.

"Heard from whom?"

Rose shrugged her thin shoulders. "Some senior girls. They weren't even talking to me."

"Then maybe you misunderstood," Keri said. If the team's new coach had suspended Bryan, which seemed far-fetched to say the least, Bryan would have told her. "Come on. Let's get going."

Rose kept pace with Keri as they hurried down the hall, a testament to how far the girl had come since the accident. Sometimes it was hard to tell her left leg had been amputated from above the knee, but Keri wasn't so sure Rose believed that.

"Is it okay if I sit with you at the game?" Rose asked in a small voice when they stopped at the hall closet. She pulled out a black pea coat and put it on.

"Sure." Keri tried not to let it show she was worried about Rose's lack of friends. "I like having you with me anytime I can get you."

Turning this way and that to view herself from different angles, Rose gazed into the full-length mirror on the back of the closet door. "Do I look all right?"

She sounded so unsure of herself that Keri ached for her. Why couldn't Rose see what Keri saw? A lovely, sweet girl who looked even better on the inside?

"You're beautiful." Keri tucked a hand under Rose's arm. "Let's get to the gym where everybody can see you."

Rose didn't speak again until they were in the driveway on opposite sides of the ten-year-old Volvo Keri had bought because of its superior safety record. Her words were so soft Keri almost didn't hear her. "You didn't have to say I was beautiful."

"I said it because I believe it," Keri assured her over the roof of the car. "But this taking an hour to get ready thing is driving me nuts."

Rose cracked a grin. "Teenagers are supposed to drive adults nuts. Bryan doesn't do it, so it's my job."

Headlights lit a swath of road in front of the house as a two-door Honda Civic pulled up to the curb. Keri's reply died on her lips. It was the same Civic Bryan had gotten a fabulous deal on from a local used-car dealer.

The car's engine cut off, and the driver's-side door opened. Bryan unfolded his tall, lanky frame from inside the car and slammed the door. Hard.

Keri went to meet him at the foot of the driveway, concern compelling her forward. "Bryan, what are you doing here?"

He moved away from his car with jerky steps, the glow from a nearby streetlight shining on his face and revealing the glisten of…tears?

"Coach Quinlan suspended me until further notice," he said gruffly, his eyelids blinking rapidly.

The gossip Rose had heard at school had been right.

"Why?" Keri asked.

"Something about my grades," he said in the same uneven voice.

"I just got your report card," Keri said. "Your grades are fine."

"I know," Bryan replied.

"Then what's going on?"

"You'll have to ask Coach Quinlan." Bryan trudged

past her up the sidewalk to the front door and disappeared through it, leaving Keri completely confused.

"Told you so." Rose's voice seemed to come from a distance. "Guess this means we're not going to the game."

"Oh, yes we are." Keri headed back to the car and got in, pulling the door shut and waiting until Rose was seated before shoving her key in the ignition. "Coach Quinlan has some explaining to do."

ALL BUT ONE OF THE PLAYERS in the locker room sat on the benches with their legs spread, their hands dangling between their knees, staring down at their high-tops as Grady delivered the postgame talk.

The exception—a tall, barrel-chested kid named Hubie Brown who was easily the second-best player on the team—openly glared at him.

The game had gone about as well as Grady expected. Springhill stayed close until the other team pulled away in the last two minutes of play, handing Springhill its first loss of the season.

Close, Grady was quickly discovering, wasn't good enough at Springhill.

"Practice is tomorrow morning at nine, so think about what I said and be ready to go." Grady spoke with authority, one of the many things he'd learned while on the coaching staff at Carolina State. Before his future had blown up in his face. "The harder we practice, the better we'll get. Okay, everybody up."

The boys reluctantly stood. Grady put his hand in the middle of an imaginary circle. A few seconds ticked by before the hands of the boys joined his.

"Let's say this together. One…" Only Grady's voice rang out in the quiet locker room. He stopped.

"Try it again," he ordered, looking at each boy in turn, few of whom looked back. "One, two, three, team."

This time all of their voices joined in, even if some were so soft they weren't audible. Grady let his hand fall, signaling the players were free to go. They pulled on black-and-gold Springhill sweat suits and picked up gym bags before filing out of the locker room. Hubie moved more slowly than the others, his silence speaking the loudest.

"Hubie, come over here," Grady said.

The boy grudgingly complied, moving toward Grady as though his feet fought quicksand. Hubie wasn't quite eye to eye with Grady but probably had fifty pounds on him, most of it muscle.

"You got something to say?" Grady asked.

The boy compressed his lips, his struggle to hold back his thoughts obvious.

"Go ahead." Grady didn't break eye contact. "We're the only ones here. I won't bench you, if that's what you're worried about."

"We'd have won with Bryan on the floor." The words burst from Hubie like water from a geyser.

"Might have won," Grady corrected.

"We lost by six and Bryan's averaging twenty. We need him, Coach."

"Then tell Bryan he's letting the team down. Tell him it's up to him when he comes back."

"You're the one who can lift the suspension. Bryan doesn't even know what you want from him."

"He knows." Grady turned away, effectively ending the conversation. He wasn't about to go into the details of his beef with Bryan with one of Bryan's peers.

Too many of Grady's own peers, from teachers at the school to fans in the stands, were demanding answers.

Grady pulled on his fleece-lined jacket, stuffed his clip-board into his gym bag and left the locker room. The game had ended thirty minutes ago, but the gym wasn't empty. The custodial staff picked up trash from the bleachers. Some parents remained, either talking to players or one another. As did a couple of cheerleaders and other girls who'd waited around for their boyfriends.

Everybody seemed to look up at once when Grady emerged, giving him the uneasy feeling that he'd be walking the gauntlet to his car.

He half expected to be accosted by an overzealous booster, but the only person headed in his direction was a young woman with wavy, shoulder-length brown hair who couldn't have been much more than twenty-one or twenty-two. She dressed older, though—in dress slacks instead of blue jeans, and a three-quarter-length brown wool coat that hid her shape. She didn't bother to hide her emotions.

"I need to talk to you." Her voice, like her manner, screamed urgency. Her color was high, somehow high-lighting the freckles sprinkled across her small nose.

She was too young to be a parent of one of the players and too old to be a girlfriend. Grady couldn't figure out what her business was with him. A girl came and stood just behind her.

Everybody else in the gym seemed equally curious. Conversation had ceased, with all eyes on them.

"Yes?" he asked expectantly.

She perched a fist on each hip. "Are you happy?"

A weird question. "My team just lost, ma'am. I'm clearly not happy."

"You'd have won if you'd played Bryan. I want to know what right you had to suspend him."

Grady should have guessed. This was about Bryan Charleton, as everything else had been this night. He curbed an urge to walk away without answering.

"Being the head coach gives me the right." He kept his voice smooth and even, betraying none of the irritation percolating inside him. "Now, if you'll excuse me."

He moved quickly toward the exit, his long strides eating up the ground until he was through the gym door and in the parking lot. He unlocked the driver's-side door of his car with his remote, looking forward to sliding inside and turning the radio way, way up. When he got home, he'd pop open a beer, put up his feet and watch *Sports Center.* After the train wreck today had been, he deserved to relax a little.

"Hey, wait a minute." The tap of heels on the pavement of the parking lot followed the sound of the woman's voice. "I'm not through talking to you."

After casting a brief, longing look at his car, he stopped and turned. She was coming so fast, she would have slammed into him had he not put out a hand to stop her.

Beneath the coat, her shoulders felt surprisingly delicate for somebody with such fierce determination on her face. He dropped his hand, but she didn't step back.

"Did you know there were college recruiters from Temple and Villanova in the stands tonight? Because of you, Bryan didn't get a chance to show them what he can do."

Grady had known about the recruiters, but in his opinion Bryan was the reason *Bryan* hadn't gotten to play in front of the scouts.

"You're wasting your time. I don't care if you're Bryan Charleton's biggest fan, I'm not talking about him with you."

"You think I'm a fan?" Her eyes, as dark as the night around them, flashed. He noticed she had the thinnest of spaces between her two front teeth.

"You're not his mother," Grady stated.

She stood up straighter, which still put her at eight or nine inches below Grady's height. "Oh, yes I am."

He took a closer look at her, noting her youngish face and smooth skin. "You can't be more than twenty-one or twenty-two."

"I'm twenty-five," she snapped. "Bryan's my adopted son. And you owe me an explanation."

He'd rather hear the story of how she'd come to adopt a teenage boy only eight years her junior, but she appeared in no mood to satisfy his curiosity.

"You'd already have had an explanation if you'd introduced yourself before you lit into me," he said. "I'm Grady Quinlan, by the way."

"I know your name."

"Yet I still don't know yours."

For the first time since she'd approached him, she looked uneasy. "Keri Cassidy."

He hadn't expected to recognize the name, but he was sure he'd heard it before. He searched his mind but couldn't place where or when.

"Well, then, Keri Cassidy, I'll tell you what I told

Bryan. I don't care how good he is, if he cheats at school, he gets suspended."

"What?" The early January air was cold enough that her breath came out in a frosty puff. "Bryan doesn't cheat."

"I say he does."

"He doesn't need to cheat. He's a good student. He's getting at least a B in every class."

"Those aren't necessarily the grades he deserves."

"That's for his teachers to decide."

"I am one of his teachers."

He could tell the information surprised her. Bryan must not have told her he'd had a teaching as well as a coaching change.

"Which class?" she asked.

"Nutrition and exercise. I took over Coach Cartwright's classes. The students are required to write papers. I have information that Bryan didn't write his."

She angled her head, and he felt as if she was trying to see inside him. "Information? From whom?"

"From the girl who wrote the paper for him, which I understand happens in his other classes, too."

"Did Bryan admit to this?"

"No."

Her head shook, rustling her hair. "Then you can't possibly know for sure it's true."

"I wouldn't have suspended him if I didn't believe it." He stamped his feet. The temperature felt to be in the twenties and dropping. His hands were cold, and he no longer had sensation in his ears.

She opened her mouth to say something else, but he stopped her. "Go home and talk to Bryan. If you have more to discuss, I'll be in my office after practice tomorrow. Noon."

She seemed about ready to protest, then a squall of wind whipped across the parking lot, blowing hair into her face. She brushed the strands back. "Oh, I'll still want to discuss it. You can count on that."

She hurried off. Despite the cold, he stared after her, noticing the same girl he'd seen with her earlier now waited in the lighted lobby of the gym. A younger sister? Another adoptive child?

He craned his neck, expecting to see a man with them, but they were alone when they emerged from the building. Keri Cassidy put her arm around the girl, as though shielding her from the world. They headed for a dark-colored Volvo across the lot from where he was parked.

Halfway there, the girl looked up and stared at him. Keri Cassidy's head lifted. He couldn't see her expression or hear what she said but knew by her body language that it wasn't good.

The wind gusted again, this time carrying a few snowflakes. Grady became aware that he hadn't moved since she left his side. He fought to keep his chin up as he walked through the wind-whipped parking lot to his car.

After what he'd been through at Carolina State, he should be used to people thinking the worst about him. But somehow, he wasn't.

CHAPTER TWO

KERI FOUND BRYAN LYING on his bed, his earphones blotting out all noise except the songs on his MP3 player.

She knocked on the open door, but he didn't sit up until she stepped into his field of vision. His eyes were no longer red, but a few balled-up tissues littered the floor near the wastebasket. He wore a Springhill High basketball T-shirt and team sweatpants.

She didn't yet have all the facts, but her heart already ached for him. She hesitated, unsure of how to proceed, which wasn't usually the way she felt around Bryan. It was how she always felt when dealing with Rose.

"Springhill lost by six," she finally told him.

Bryan indicated the sleek black cell phone beside him on the bed. "I know. Hubie text messaged. He told me about the college scouts."

Keri nodded. The verification seemed to make him feel worse. He hung his head, his expression dejected. Keri had never seen Bryan like this before.

If not for basketball, Keri might have worried that the easygoing Bryan would let life pass him by. But on court, he turned into a fierce competitor.

"Can I sit down?" she asked.

He moved over, making room for her on the extralong bed she'd special-ordered so his feet wouldn't hang over the end.

His bedroom couldn't have been more different from Rose's. Everything had a place, from the neat rows of books on his bookshelf to the stacks of CDs behind his bed. He'd replaced the posters of NBA stars that used to adorn his walls with an assortment of excellent photographs he'd taken himself, but left in place shelves crowded with basketball trophies.

"I talked to Coach Quinlan after the game," Keri said.

Bryan let out a harsh sound, making it very clear what he thought of his basketball coach. Keri was still making up her mind. Aside from his height, the coach hadn't looked the way she'd expected him to. With short brown hair that sprang back from his forehead in thick waves, high cheekbones and clear hazel eyes, he resembled a grown-up version of the All-American boy. But she had enough sense not to judge the caliber of a man by the strength of his good looks.

"I didn't know Coach Quinlan was one of your teachers," she continued.

"Lucky me," Bryan muttered under his breath, his sarcasm heavy and uncharacteristic.

"He said he suspended you because someone else wrote the paper you turned in."

Bryan spun toward her, his dark eyes wide. He looked so much like his mother at that moment that Keri's breath caught. "And you believe I'd do something like that?"

She didn't. Rose hadn't been far off when she'd remarked that Bryan didn't drive Keri crazy. In the three years since she'd become their guardian and later their adoptive mother, Keri had few complaints. Oh, Bryan sometimes forgot to phone and let her know where he was. And he'd arrived home after curfew more than once. But overall, he was a very good kid.

"I didn't say I believed it," Keri said slowly, "but I would like to hear your side of the story."

"I wrote my own paper. That's my side."

"Then why does Coach Quinlan think someone else wrote it?"

"Because Becky Harding is mad I didn't ask her to the Snowball Dance."

"Becky Harding?" Keri tried to remember if he'd mentioned the girl before but couldn't place her name. So many girls congregated around Bryan that Keri couldn't even recall the name of the tall, willowy blonde he'd taken to the dance. "Who's she?"

"Some cheerleader who has a thing for me. We hung out a couple of times, sure, but she made too much of it."

"So this Becky Harding, she told Coach Quinlan she wrote your paper?"

"Yeah, but she can't prove it. It wasn't handwritten or anything."

"So why didn't you offer to show him the saved document on your computer?"

"Becky told him she sent it to me electronically, then erased it."

Bryan had given the impression he'd just found out about the suspension when he showed up at the house before game time, but he seemed to know an awful lot about the details.

"Bryan, when did Coach Quinlan suspend you?" Keri asked.

He answered her immediately. "At school today."

"Then why didn't you tell me about it?"

"Because the charges are bogus. I thought Coach would realize that and let me play. I just don't get him." Bryan made a noise and shook his head. "Must be on some kind of power trip."

Keri tried to make sense of that. "But if the story's not true, what motive would he have to suspend his best player?"

"To prove he's a hard-ass," Bryan retorted.

Keri slanted him a look rich with disapproval.

"Sorry," Bryan said quickly. "I meant he's one of those tough guys who won't change his mind no matter what."

"And you think he's made up his mind about you?"

"He believed Becky Harding, didn't he?"

"Did you tell him your side?"

"Hell, y— I mean, yes, ma'am. But he wouldn't listen. He has this chip on his shoulder, like he has something to prove."

"What can he possibly prove without his best player on the floor?"

"That he's such a good coach he can win with anybody in the lineup."

The logic seemed skewed to Keri, but then she couldn't relate to the Grady Quinlans of the world. "I'll talk to him again tomorrow after practice."

Bryan didn't say anything for a few moments. "How 'bout if I ask Mr. Marco to be there, too?"

At the name of the school's athletic director, Keri felt her muscles tense. "I didn't realize you and Mr. Marco had that close of a relationship."

"Me, neither," Bryan said. "But he told me at the beginning of the season to come to him if I needed anything. He even gave me his cell number."

"I don't think—"

"Please, Keri," Bryan pleaded, leaning closer to her. She smelled the body spray he'd started to use when he noticed girls noticing him. "Mr. Marco will be on our side."

She hesitated, but Bryan gazed at her so beseechingly that in the end there was only one answer she could give. "Okay."

She tried to return Bryan's grateful smile, but her mind was already preoccupied with tomorrow's meeting. She couldn't say which of the two men she looked less forward to dealing with.

Grady Quinlan, the basketball coach who thought he had the right to ruin Bryan's future. Or Tony Marco, the man to whom Keri might have pledged her own future if he hadn't unexpectedly broken their engagement.

HANDS LOCKED BEHIND HIS back, Grady watched the Springhill High players finish the last of the line sprints that usually signaled the end of practice.

The more free throws they missed during the two hours of practice, the more they ran.

Bryan Charleton, the best free-throw shooter on the team, usually loudly urged his teammates to follow his example as he sank shot after shot.

Bryan hadn't shown up for practice today.

The soles of basketball shoes squeaked over the court, then silenced, the only sounds the harsh inhales and exhales as the players fought to get their breathing to return to normal. Some of the boys bent at the waist, sweat trickling down their faces and dripping to the floor. Others, their arms folded above their heads so their elbows angled outward, started to file toward the locker room.

"Not so fast." Grady's voice rang out in the gym. "Give me one more. Hubie and Sam, touch every line this time or we'll do it again."

Groans drowned out the heavy breathing.

"You've got to be kidding me," Hubie groused.

"Make that two more," Grady said. "Anybody got anything else to say?"

Nobody did. Eleven of the twelve members of the Springhill High varsity lined up shoulder to shoulder on the baseline, some of them red-faced, all of them damp with perspiration. Grady ignored the internal voice that told him to give the kids a break.

Coaches used to refer to the drill they were about to repeat as "suicides" before the term was deemed politically incorrect. The players were required to sprint to the near foul line, the half-court line, the far foul line and the far baseline, bending to touch each line in turn before returning to their starting place.

This time every player touched every line, although a couple of the boys looked ready to collapse when they finished.

"We've got tomorrow off so I'll see you Monday," Grady said, then left the court before another team member had a chance to say something Grady would have to make him regret.

Only then did he notice Keri Cassidy, who lingered near the door that led to the athletic offices.

She'd dressed more her age today, in blue jeans and a quilted blue jacket, her hair falling to her shoulders in loose waves. She appeared to be wearing little or no makeup, a fresh-faced look he found appealing.

"Did you have to be so hard on them?" she asked when he was close enough that she didn't have to shout.

She might not look like a mom, but she sure sounded like one.

He considered telling her that, contrary to popular opinion, he didn't enjoy being the bad guy. That he'd embraced the roll for the good of the young men on his team.

But she wouldn't understand, not if she'd come here to defend Bryan Charleton.

"Yeah," he said, and walked past her to the door. He held it open, nodding across the wide hallway to his office. "We can talk there."

The office was the same one Fuzz Cartwright had used for the twenty-two years he'd been head basketball coach at Springhill. Grady watched Keri's eyes travel over the interior walls—painted gold, of course—that Cartwright had decorated with photos of district championship teams and Coach of the Year plaques.

"Have a seat." Grady indicated one of two chairs across from the worn wood desk. He sat behind the desk. His usual style was considerably less formal, but he had a strong feeling that Keri Cassidy was about to challenge his authority.

Deciding it was to his advantage to get in the first word, he asked, "Any idea why Bryan wasn't at practice?"

"Because you suspended him." She seemed to think the answer was obvious.

"He's part of the team. He's supposed to come to practice."

"Did you tell him that?" He wouldn't call the narrow-eyed way she regarded him a glare, exactly, but it was close. Grady seldom noted eye color but her eyes were green. "Because how's a kid who's never been suspended before supposed to know the rules?"

"Everybody knows the rules."

"I don't. Bryan obviously doesn't."

Grady wasn't ready to concede that Bryan's absence had been innocent, but this line of conversation wasn't getting them anywhere. "What did Bryan say when you asked him about the paper?"

"He says he—"

Three short raps on the frame of the open door interrupted her reply. His cousin Tony entered the office as though he'd been invited. In chinos, a long-sleeved black polo shirt the color of his hair and a fresh shave, he looked far better than he did most Saturday mornings. He turned to Keri with an apologetic shrug. "Sorry I'm late."

Grady addressed Keri, not hiding his surprise. "You asked Tony to be here?"

"Bryan asked," Keri replied, eyes on Grady instead of Tony.

Tony sat down, inching his chair marginally closer to Keri's. "I'm happy to help you anytime I can, Keri."

Two against one, Grady thought. His cousin had already made it known how he felt about the suspension. Grady's eyes fell on his cousin's hand, resting on the arm of Keri's chair. But how did Tony feel about Keri?

"K—" Grady stopped himself from using her first name, realized he didn't know whether or not she was married and glanced at the ring finger of her left hand.

Bare. "Ms. Cassidy was about to tell me what Bryan said about cheating."

"He said he didn't cheat." Her reply was immediate, her tone sharp.

No surprise there.

"He said the girl who accused him has a grudge against him." She firmed her chin. "And I believe him."

"I think the issue is why Grady believes the girl," Tony said, as if his was the voice of reason. When his cousin confronted him about this very issue before last night's game, Grady got the distinct impression Tony didn't care why Grady believed Bryan was guilty. Or even if Bryan was guilty.

"The girl told me what Web sites she used as source material," Grady said.

"That's it?" Keri asked, expressive eyes wide and disbelieving. "That's all the proof you have?"

"That's not all." He leveled her with the stare that caused his players to flinch. She didn't move a muscle. "I asked Bryan questions about what was in the paper, and he couldn't answer."

"Now, I don't want to take sides here," Tony said, "but isn't it possible Bryan didn't retain the information? The paper was about nutrition, right? I can't even remember the five food groups."

Grady crossed his arms over his chest. "You didn't just write a paper about them."

"True. But you haven't been teaching at Springhill long. I know the personalities better than you do."

Unswayed, Grady said nothing.

"C'mon, man," Tony said. "I'm telling you Bryan's all

right. You and me go back far enough that you can trust my judgment."

Keri turned her head to gaze at Tony, the first time she'd looked directly at him since he entered the office. "You knew Coach Quinlan before he started teaching at the school?"

"Remember I told you I had a cousin who played college ball?" Tony phrased the question as though he'd told Keri a lot of things. As though they had the type of relationship where they shared confidences. "Grady's that cousin."

"Isn't there some rule against hiring a relative?"

"Not that I know of," Tony said. "Even if there was, this is a special case. We needed somebody fast after Coach Cartwright had the heart attack. We're lucky Grady was available."

It sounded to Grady as though Tony was trying to justify his decision. The knowledge rankled, but not as much as the disapproval would once the relationship between Grady and the athletic director got out. Grady wondered if Keri Cassidy would be the one to spread the word.

"Where'd you play?" Keri asked.

Grady didn't usually avoid direct questions, but since the scandal he preferred not to talk about Carolina State. "I didn't play. I sat the bench and watched."

"Perfect training for a coach," Tony interjected.

"A good coach knows as much about his players as he does basketball," Keri said. "Did you know Bryan lost his mother in a car accident? Playing basketball got him through it. It's his dream to play in college."

Grady hadn't known about Bryan's mother, but he'd

only been coach of the Springhill varsity for a little more than two weeks. In truth, he had as many questions about how Keri had ended up adopting Bryan as he did about Bryan. Steeling himself against the plea in her eyes to go easier on her child, he said, "Then he shouldn't have cheated on that paper."

She opened her mouth, probably to leap again to Bryan's defense, but Tony spoke first.

"We seem to have reached an impasse," Tony said. "But since the team needs Bryan as much as Bryan needs the team, why don't we compromise? Grady, how about letting Bryan play if he turns in another paper?"

"If Bryan doesn't turn in another paper—handwritten, so I know he did the work himself—he'll flunk the class," Grady said.

Keri edged forward in her seat. "What about the suspension? Is it indefinite?"

"He turns in the paper, he can play in the game this coming Friday. That was my plan all along."

"Friday? What about Tuesday?" Keri asked. Springhill typically played twice a week, and the Cougars' next game was at home Tuesday night.

"Friday," Grady repeated. "I want to impress upon him how serious the offense is."

"You can't even be sure he cheated!"

"I'm sure." He clenched his jaw. "And I'm not going to discuss it anymore. I've made up my mind."

Her face flushed. "But you—"

"You heard the man, Keri," Tony interrupted. "Take it from me. When Grady digs in his feet, there's nothing that'll unearth him."

In other words, Grady thought, Tony didn't agree with him, either. Too bad. Tony had entrusted Grady to do what was right. Standing firm on Bryan's punishment was right.

Tony got to his feet and smoothed down the front of his chinos. "You'll tell Bryan what we decided. Right, Keri?"

She waited a few sullen beats before she replied, "Right."

"Then let me walk you to your car," Tony offered.

Keri sat rigidly in the chair, saying nothing. Grady supposed he could attribute her stiff posture to simmering anger toward him, but he didn't think that was the only reason.

After a lengthy pause, Keri stood up and preceded Tony out of the office. Tony touched her on the shoulder as she passed by. Had Grady not been watching carefully, he would have missed Keri subtly shrugging off Tony's hand.

Something was going on between Keri and his cousin, he concluded. And he was curious to know what it was.

KERI LEFT THE COACH'S office, barely conscious of placing one foot in front of the other, her mind on the thing she most wanted to say to the almighty Coach Grady Quinlan.

You're an ass for not believing Bryan. Bryan had been through so much—he and Rose—surely he'd never lie about something like this.

"That went okay," Tony said.

"Which part?" Keri retorted. "When he called Bryan a liar? Or when he said Bryan couldn't play in the game Tuesday?"

"Look at it this way. It's not a district game, so it won't hurt our play-off chances." Tony didn't need to explain that only games against district opponents counted in the standings. "And it's only one more game."

"A game your cousin could let Bryan play if he chose."

"True," Tony said. "I see you're not a fan of Grady's."

"I don't imagine he has many of those. Arrogance isn't an attractive trait."

"He's not so bad."

"He's worse," Keri muttered.

"I'm surprised you didn't tell him that. You've never been one to hold back your opinions." He made the observations casually, as though he knew her inside and out. The way he had three years ago.

Before he'd dumped her.

They were nearly to the door leading to the parking lot. She stopped. "I don't need you to walk me to my car, Tony."

"I know that." He smiled at her in the way that used to set her heart racing. "But I want to. You've said more to me in the past five minutes than you have in the past few years."

That wasn't exactly true. Springhill had a population of fifteen thousand, small enough that town residents ran into one another from time to time. Especially when the basketball player living in the house of one of the residents starred at the school where the other person served as athletic director.

"I've never tried to avoid you, Tony," Keri said.

"You haven't gone out of your way to talk to me, either."

"Do you blame me?" As soon as she asked the question, she wished she could take it back. She'd gotten over Tony Marco a long time ago. "Forget I said that. What's past is past."

"That's just it. We never did resolve things. We shouldn't have left it the way we did." Tony positioned his body between Keri and the door, then lowered his voice. "Meet me for a drink tonight, Keri. Please."

Once upon a time Keri couldn't have refused Tony anything, but she'd grown up in the three years since he'd cast her off. Becoming a mother to two children who depended upon her and her alone had taught her she couldn't afford to spend time on somebody like Tony.

"No, Tony. I won't meet you," she said.

He was already standing too close, but moved a step closer, as though his very presence could convince her to change her mind. He smelled of the same aftershave he'd used when they were dating. Unaffected by the familiar scent, she moved a step back.

"I won't stop asking until you say yes," Tony said.

"Then your voice will get hoarse."

He moved forward again. "C'mon, Keri. You don't mean—"

"Tony."

At the sound of his name, Tony sprang away from her. Grady Quinlan strode toward them, stopped a few paces away and slowly slid his gaze from Keri to Tony. She fought to keep from squirming under his inspection. She wasn't the one who had anything to feel guilty about.

"I hope I'm not interrupting," Grady said.

"Of course not." Even to Keri, Tony's denial sounded unconvincing. Tony cleared his throat, then addressed his cousin. "What is it?"

"Mary Lynn just called looking for you. She didn't get an answer when she tried your cell."

Mary Lynn, Tony's wife. Whom he'd married six months after he'd broken things off with Keri.

Keri watched Tony's throat muscles constrict as he swallowed. "Reception's bad in this building."

"That's what I told Mary Lynn," Grady said. "Anyway, she wants you to call home."

"I will," Tony said, then nodded toward the exit. "I was just leaving. Keri? Are you coming?"

She hesitated, reluctant to subject herself to more of Tony's company.

"Before you go, Tony, I need to talk to you," Grady said, saving Keri from dreaming up an excuse not to walk out of the building with his cousin.

"Uh, sure." Tony's syllables were thick with reluctance.

"Then I'll be going," Keri said, before moving quickly toward the double doors and escape.

Before she reached the exit, she glanced over her shoulder. Tony stood with his back to her, but she had an unimpeded view of Grady, who seemed like the more commanding of the two men even though he wore gym shorts and a T-shirt. He gave her a slight, almost imperceptible nod.

She could have sworn in that moment that he realized she'd been having trouble getting Tony to take no for an answer and had come to her aid.

She dismissed the fleeting thought. She wasn't ready to give Grady Quinlan the benefit of the doubt.

About anything.

CHAPTER THREE

MONDAY MORNING ARRIVED far too soon for Keri, the same way as always. Bryan, true to form, got ready for school in about fifteen minutes flat.

"I'm leaving, Rose," she heard him call up the stairs to his younger sister. "Want a ride to school?"

"Can't you wait?" Rose yelled back. She could be heard dashing about her room.

Bryan stuck his head into the kitchen, where Keri was packing a honey-ham-and-Swiss-cheese sandwich into a brown paper bag. Rose didn't like the school cafeteria food but was running too late to make her own lunch. Keri didn't mind doing it for her, and she wanted to be sure Rose wouldn't skip eating altogether.

"Bye, Keri," Bryan said.

"Do you have that paper for Coach Quinlan?" She had little doubt the coach would not be forgiving should Bryan forget it.

"In my backpack," Bryan said, already moving toward the door. A few moments later, she heard the engine of his car start and the slide of tires over pavement as he pulled out of the driveway.

Keri finished packing Rose's lunch, checked the clock, then yelled, "Rosie, you'll miss the bus if you don't hurry."

"Can you drive me?" Rose called back.

The high school was across town in the opposite direction of the newspaper, which meant Keri would get to work a few minutes past the time she preferred to arrive.

None of her coworkers cared if she came in a few minutes late, but Keri did. To assuage her conscience, she'd either eat a quick lunch at her desk or stay late.

"Okay," Keri hollered. "But I still want you to speed it up."

Keri didn't sit down in front of her computer in the advertising department of the *Springhill Gazette* until fifteen minutes past the hour, not entirely due to Rose.

A reporter, a security guard and one of the mailroom staff had stopped her on the way to the elevator to complain about Bryan's suspension.

"New coach don't have much sense." Chester, the security guard, was a big burly man who'd played basketball for Springhill fifteen years ago. "Everybody knows Bryan's cool."

Everybody except Grady Quinlan.

Keri had swallowed her resentment and formed a diplomatic response. "It was just an unfortunate misunderstanding."

"Then Bryan's playing tomorrow night?" Chester asked.

"Friday night," she replied.

"Damn fool coach."

She relegated Chester's astute comment to the back of her mind and navigated her mouse until her twenty-one-inch flat-screen monitor showed a page from the special advertising section she'd started to lay out last Friday.

The biggest sale of the year, she typed into a text box. Wasn't that the way of the world, she thought. Everything cost less after the holiday shopping season.

"Morning, Keri." Jill McMann approached from behind her and set a fragrant cup of cappuccino on the desk next to Keri's computer. Mocha, her favorite flavor.

Keri breathed in the familiar scent, then smiled at her friend. "You're too good to me."

"Then it's your turn." Jill swept a hand down the lime-green sweater dress that looked great with her short black hair and pale skin. "Tell me you still can't see my baby weight."

"What baby weight?"

"Good answer." Jill sank into her seat at the computer in the cubicle across from Keri's.

Because Jill had filled Maddy's position after Maddy died, Keri hadn't been prepared to like her. But Jill had slowly won Keri over with her wry wit. It helped that Jill didn't like sports and never talked basketball, two things Keri got enough of at home.

"I'll deny this if you repeat it, but I'm glad I don't have to change any more diapers until tonight. I swear Amy's going for a world record." Only a year older than Keri's twenty-five, Jill had packed a lot of living into the past three years. She'd fallen in love, gotten married and had a baby girl who was now five months old. "So now that you've heard what I did this weekend, what did you do?"

"The usual. Laundry. Grocery shopping. Cleaning. Oh, and I helped Rose with a history project. She remembered on Sunday that it was due today."

"That's not what I meant," Jill said as she logged on to her computer. "Did you do anything for *you?*"

"I saw a movie."

"Now we're getting somewhere." Jill gave Keri her full attention, her amber-colored eyes sparkling. "Which movie?"

"Romancing the Stone."

Jill groaned. "That movie's twenty years old. I thought you went out to the movie theater. Possibly with a man."

"I don't have time to date," Keri said.

"You don't *make* time to date." Jill swiveled in her seat and crossed one long leg over the other. "Why, even Bryan's dating. Did I tell you I saw him at Mario's Pizza double-dating with Becky Harding and her boyfriend?"

Keri snapped to attention. "When?"

"Let's see." Jill tapped the end of a pen on her desk. "Over Christmas break. The Saturday before last."

That didn't make sense. The Snowball Dance had been before the break. If Becky was upset about not going with Bryan, why would she be hanging out with him? "Are you sure?"

"Positive. That Saturday was Kevin's birthday. He got to choose the restaurant. Last year he picked La Fontaine, that fabulous French place about an hour from here." Jill carried on, unaware she'd temporarily lost Keri's attention. "But this year we had Amy so he settled for Mario's. Good thing, too, because she started screaming bloody murder when the waiter brought the food. Probably because she doesn't have teeth yet."

"Are you positive it was Becky Harding?"

Jill seemed taken aback by the question. "Yeah. I know Becky. The Hardings are neighbors of mine."

"And Bryan was with her?"

"Not 'with her' with her," Jill said. "Bryan was with some blonde. Becky was with her boyfriend. Jeremiah something or other."

"Jeremiah Bowden," Keri supplied. She didn't know the boy personally but had heard Bryan mention his name several times.

"That's it. Jeremiah Bowden. I remember Becky's mom saying he's on the football team."

"What's Becky like?" Keri asked.

"I couldn't say, really. But I like her mom and her younger sister's a sweetie. Her sister babysits Amy sometimes." Jill slanted Keri a probing look. "Why all the questions?"

"No reason." Keri squirmed in her seat, uncomfortable at the suspicious direction her thoughts had headed. Bryan would have a perfectly logical explanation for hanging out with Becky Harding. "I just like to know who Bryan's dating."

"You're the one who should be dating. Have I told you that you need to get out more?"

"Hmm, maybe once or twice," Keri joked. "And I do get out. I'm going to Bryan's basketball game tomorrow night."

"Like you'll find an eligible man there," Jill complained.

Keri pictured Grady Quinlan and wondered if a female had laid claim to him. Disgusted with herself, she shook off her curiosity. So what if the coach was good-looking enough to stop hearts? If Keri were to start dating again, she'd choose a man whose character she could admire.

That wasn't Grady Quinlan, even if he had extricated her from that awkward situation with Tony.

"I don't go to Bryan's games to find men," Keri said.

"I know. I know. You go to watch Bryan."

Usually Jill's comment would have been spot-on, but Bryan wasn't even playing Tuesday night. Keri would go to the game, though, and not only to support the team.

She intended to get to the bottom of the Becky Harding mystery and to find out exactly why the girl had made so much trouble for Bryan. Even if she had to ask Becky herself.

MARY LYNN MARCO EXITED the kitchen of the split-level house she shared with her husband carrying two dessert plates with extralarge pieces of tiramisu.

"Here you go." The smile she'd worn the entire evening didn't waver as she put dessert plates decorated with showy flowers in front of Grady and Tony.

"Thanks," said Tony without much enthusiasm.

"You're welcome," Mary Lynn answered in kind.

Grady picked up a fork and tried to look like he wasn't about to burst from the extra helpings of rigatoni, bread and steamed vegetables she'd kept offering. "Is this the recipe you got from Uncle Vinny?"

Mary Lynn had phoned Grady over the weekend to invite him to dinner, claiming the single day he'd spent with the extended family in Johnstown over the Christmas holidays hadn't been enough. She told him she'd be using recipes she'd talked Tony's father into surrendering.

"Yes," Mary Lynn said. "It's layers of Italian sponge cake and mascarpone cream, although Tony's dad's tiramisu looks a lot better than mine."

"Looks pretty good to me," Grady said.

Mary Lynn adopted an even bigger smile, then sat down at the end of the table across from Tony and next to Grady. "I'm so happy you came tonight, Grady. Any cousin of Tony's is always welcome here."

Tony caught Grady's eyes and raised his eyebrows. "You already told him that, Mary Lynn. Three times."

Mary Lynn's smile wavered, but only slightly. She was such a champion smiler she would have done well on the beauty pageant circuit. With her long curly blond hair, blue eyes and delicate features, she was certainly pretty enough. She was twenty-four, but seemed younger, partly because she was about five foot two.

She made an odd couple with the much more serious Tony, but Grady didn't know how they'd hooked up. He and Tony had grown up on opposite ends of Pennsylvania, seeing each other at the occasional family get-togethers as children and even less frequently as adults.

"I'll never get tired of you saying I'm welcome here," Grady told Mary Lynn. "I like hearing how much you two enjoy my company."

"Mary Lynn's speaking for herself," Tony said, his fork full of tiramisu suspended halfway to his mouth. "You made my life a living hell this past week by suspending Bryan Charleton."

"You're not going to start talking about that basketball player again, are you?" Mary Lynn even smiled when she was complaining. "Isn't it enough that he's back on the team?"

"Not when R.G. won't let him play Tuesday," Tony said.

"If Grady won't let him play, he probably wants to make real sure the boy learns his lesson," Mary Lynn said.

Grady slanted Mary Lynn a grateful look. "Exactly right."

Tony's dark eyebrows arched as he addressed Grady. "The way you learned a lesson from what happened at Carolina State?"

Grady felt as though Tony had cut into his flesh, then taken the shaker from the table and liberally sprinkled salt into his wound. "The two have nothing to do with each other."

"Sure they do," Tony said. "Right about now Bryan thinks life isn't fair. Isn't that how you felt when you couldn't get another job coaching basketball?"

Did Tony honestly think Grady had tried to get another coaching job? Grady assumed Tony knew he'd been driving a truck by choice. Well, maybe choice was the wrong word. It certainly hadn't taken much convincing for Tony to talk him into applying for the teaching position at Springhill.

"I didn't look for another coaching job," Grady said. "You came to me when Fuzz had the heart attack, remember?"

Mary Lynn laid a hand on Grady's forearm. "And he's told me a dozen times how lucky Springhill is to have you. Isn't that right, Tony?"

"Yeah," Tony said. "But I still wish he hadn't suspended Bryan."

Tony brought the tiramisu the rest of the way to his mouth. Grady dug in, too. The bitter, grainy taste of strong coffee hit him at the same time Tony reached for a half-empty glass of water beside his plate and drained it.

"What's the matter?" Mary Lynn asked. "Did I mess up the recipe?"

"It's fine," Tony said, although it obviously wasn't.

"I think you used coffee grounds instead of brewed coffee," Grady told her.

"I'm so sorry." She stood up and gathered up their plates with the barely eaten tiramisu. She blinked a few times, Grady thought to keep from crying. "I'll clean up."

When Mary Lynn was gone, Grady asked Tony in a quiet voice, "Don't you want to make sure she's all right?"

"She'll be fine," Tony said.

Grady wasn't so sure, an observation that was proved true when he carried some dirty dishes into the kitchen and found Mary Lynn wiping tears from under her eyes.

He patted her awkwardly on the back. "Don't cry, Mary Lynn. It's only dessert."

"That's not why I'm crying." She blinked a few times. "Did you hear how polite Tony is around me? He couldn't even tell me the tiramisu was awful." Mary Lynn took a tissue out of the box and dabbed at her eyes. "Listen to me. Blabbing to you about my troubles. And you being Tony's cousin."

Grady's desire to help Mary Lynn overrode his vaguely uncomfortable feeling at hearing her private business. "I'm family. Anything you tell me stays with me."

"You're a sweetheart," she said, blinking up at him through damp eyelashes. "It's just that I've been trying to get pregnant for almost a year, and I can't get Tony to go to an infertility clinic." She sniffed. "Sometimes I think it's because he doesn't want to have a baby with me."

Grady would have issued a consoling statement if he hadn't gotten the distinct impression that Tony had been hitting on Keri Cassidy, not the sign of a happily married man.

"I'm sorry." Mary Lynn covered her mouth, her hand trembling, her expression miserable. "You'd think that after being married two years, I still wouldn't be so jealous of her."

"Of who?" Grady asked.

"Tony's ex. You know he was engaged before he married me, right?"

Grady nodded, although he'd never met Tony's fiancé. He'd been too busy trying to build a successful team at Carolina State.

"It's hard living in the same town as her," Mary Lynn said on a heavy sigh.

The same town…

"What's her name?" he asked.

Mary Lynn took a shuddering breath before she replied, but Grady already knew what her answer would be. It was why the name had seemed familiar to him.

"Keri Cassidy," she said.

KERI STOOD ABOUT TEN FEET from the baseline Tuesday night, close enough to the Springhill High cheerleading squad that she had to guard against getting whacked in the face by a black-and-gold pom-pom.

At a few minutes past game time, every seat in the gym seemed to be taken. Keri's only hope was if the group of parents she usually sat with saved her a seat.

"Watch out!" The tiny, dark-haired cheerleader at the end of the line shouted a warning.

Keri turned toward the court to see a player in black-and-gold valiantly trying to save the basketball from going out of bounds. He caught his balance before she could move out of the way, nimbly stepping between Keri and the cheerleader.

That's when Keri realized who he was: Bryan.

He winked at her before running back on court, leaving her staring openmouthed after him. Against all odds, Coach Quinlan was letting him play.

The cheerleaders continued with their go-fight-win cheer, nearly deafening Keri. She looked toward the bleachers again and spotted an upraised hand waving wildly. It belonged to Lori Patterson, the mother of the senior point guard.

She headed up the aisle that cut through the bleachers, with fans craning their necks to see around her. Lori sat on the end beside the center aisle. She scooted over, creating nearly enough space for one person. Keri sat down, a portion of her right hip hanging over only slightly into the aisle.

"Hey, there." Lori squeezed Keri's knee. Short and compact with a fabulous complexion, she was about fifteen years older than Keri. But then, so were all the other parents, a fact that had once made Keri uncomfortable. Now she was used to it. "Where's Rosie?"

"I couldn't get her to come," Keri said.

Lori nodded, her heart-shaped face full of understanding. Lori was divorced so usually came to the games alone, a reason Keri had gravitated toward her. They only socialized at basketball games but had become friends, sharing stories about their problems and triumphs with their children.

"She's missing a show. Bryan already has six points," Lori said, her face bright with excitement. Keri did a quick check of the scoreboard, noting that Springhill was up 10-8.

"Great steal, Garrett," Lori yelled at the top of her lungs, calling out her son's name. On court the wiry point guard had a two-on-one break, with Bryan running the lane adjacent to him. The defender committed to Garrett, who bounced a pass to Bryan. Bryan caught the ball in stride, took a long step and elevated over the rim. Holding the ball in one large hand, he thrust it through the rim.

The crowd went wild.

From the home team's bench, Grady Quinlan, in a black dress shirt and gold tie, yelled something at Bryan. By the coach's expansive gestures, it wasn't something positive. The guy probably thought dunking was equivalent to showboating.

Unbelievable.

Maybe more mind-boggling was Keri's expectation that reversing his decision to play Bryan would turn Grady into a kinder and gentler coach.

Yeah, right.

"It's gonna be a close game," Lori said breathlessly. "Westlake's supposed to win their district, too."

Lori's comment proved prophetic—Springhill was leading by only two points at the half.

"Good thing for Springhill Bryan's playing tonight," Lori said, a huge smile wreathing her face.

"He should have played Friday night, too." The speaker was Hubie Brown's mother, Carolyn, who sat on the other side of Lori. A large woman who always dressed in bright colors, she never kept her opinions to herself. "I bet Coach Quinlan feels stupid for losing that game after what happened in school today."

Lori's head bobbed in agreement, as though whatever happened was common knowledge.

"What happened?" Keri asked.

Carolyn smoothed the sleeve of her orange sweater and widened her eyes. "Didn't Bryan tell you?"

"I haven't talked to Bryan since this morning," Keri admitted. Her son left for the gym before she arrived home on game days because he liked to watch the junior varsity, which played before the varsity.

"Wait till you hear this." Carolyn leaned closer, nearly knocking Lori over. "Becky Harding admitted she lied. Just came straight out and told Quinlan she made it all up."

That explained Grady Quinlan's uncharacteristic change of heart. He'd been forced to soften his stance.

"That's great," Keri said, but something didn't add up. "But why would Becky admit to that?"

"Guess guilt was eating her up," Carolyn suggested. "Maybe embarrassment, too. Everybody found out she had a thing for Bryan."

"That's something else that doesn't make sense," Keri said. "I heard she's dating one of the football players."

Carolyn slanted Keri a significant look and patted her on the hand. "You're so young sometimes, Keri. If you can't have the one you love, you love the one you're with."

Maybe, Keri thought. But if Becky was so resentful of Bryan, why had she been hanging out with him a few days after the Snowball Dance? Keri had asked Bryan that very question last night, and he'd shrugged it off. A chance meeting, he'd called it.

"Oh, look!" Lori pointed to a group of lithe young girls in black unitards who were running lightly onto the court, their toes pointed like ballerinas. "The dance team. I just love watching them."

Loud music with a rap beat sounded over the public address system. Before Lori could get too entranced with the dancers, Keri leaned over and asked close to her friend's ear, "Do you know which of the cheerleaders is Becky?"

Her attention focused on the smiling, dancing girls, Lori answered, "Sure do. The shortest one. Long, dark hair. Bangs. Sets up on the end."

The very cheerleader who'd given Keri a heads-up when Bryan had come flying out of bounds. Keri scanned the gym for black-and-gold uniforms, locating the majority of the cheerleaders near the doors leading to the snack bar.

"Save my seat," Keri told Lori, then descended the bleachers and walked directly to where Becky chatted with one of her squad members.

"Becky."

The girl turned around, a puzzled expression on her pretty face as she tilted her chin to gaze up at Keri. Keri was of average height, but Becky wasn't much more than five feet tall. Keri smelled the peppermint scent of the gum Becky was chewing.

"Yes?" Becky asked expectantly, a half smile on her face.

"I'm Keri Cassidy." Most people in Springhill knew Keri had adopted Bryan and Rose after Maddy's fatal accident, but Becky didn't seem to be one of them. "Bryan Charleton's mom."

Becky's smile vanished, her jaws stopped working on the gum and her posture turned rigid.

"If you're here to ask me about that nutrition paper, I already took care of it," she said in clipped tones.

"I heard you told Coach Quinlan you lied about writing it."

Becky's wary expression didn't change but she said nothing.

"Why did you say you wrote the paper in the first place?" Keri persisted.

"It doesn't matter," Becky said, chomping down on her gum. "Bryan's playing tonight. Isn't that what everybody wanted?"

"Of course it mat—" Keri said, but Becky had already turned away, obviously having said all she was going to say.

Taken aback by the girl's rudeness, Keri clenched her jaw. She thought about tapping the girl on the shoulder again, but creating a scene wouldn't get her answers. She started back to her seat, nearly bumping into a woman with long, curly blond hair who was holding a foil-wrapped hot dog and a bottle of water. Mary Lynn Marco, Tony's wife.

Their eyes met. Before Keri could say hello or even smile, Mary Lynn walked quickly past her, as though being chased by a hellhound. So much for letting the other woman in on the long-overdue fact that Keri wished her only the best of luck with Tony.

The half started almost as soon as Keri reached her bleacher seat, giving her little time to dwell on either Becky's comments or Mary Lynn's coolness. The two teams played at a breathtaking pace, exchanging baskets and the lead.

Keri had seen Bryan play basketball many times, but still marveled over how a boy who was so laid-back off the court could be so intense on it.

When Bryan got the ball at the three-point line with thirty seconds left and Springhill trailing by four, Keri knew the shot would be good even before the ball left his fingertips. The three-pointer brought Springhill within one, sending the crowd into hysterics.

"I can hardly stand how exciting this is," Lori said, literally on the edge of her seat.

Westlake successfully inbounded the ball to its point guard, who dribbled up the court. From two seats away, Carolyn yelled, "Steal the ball."

When the opposing point guard attempted to get the ball to a teammate, Bryan did exactly that, swooping into a passing lane out of seemingly nowhere to grab the ball out of the air. He raced down court, with two Westlake players hounding his every stride. The crowd roared as the clock ticked down to ten seconds.

Instead of forcing a shot when he was well defended, Bryan alertly passed to a teammate open under the basket. Joey Jividen. One of the younger boys on the varsity, Joey had entered the game when another player fouled out.

With nobody guarding him, Joey had an easy two points. The ball left his hand with plenty of time to spare. It banked off the glass, rattled around the hoop and rimmed out.

One of the opposing players grabbed the rebound but lost his footing and stepped on the end line. The referee blew the whistle, signaling possession would go to Springhill. The clock showed five seconds left to play.

"Time-out," Grady yelled, forming his hands into a T.

The Springhill side of the crowd was silent, seemingly in shock. "How could you miss that gimme, Jividen?"

A guy with a booming voice yelled from somewhere behind Keri.

"I'll tell you how," Carolyn Brown muttered. "Joey's not very good. He shouldn't even be on the court."

"I think Joey does fine," Keri said.

Carolyn harrumphed.

The Springhill players walked back to the huddle, with Joey at the rear, hanging his head.

Keri expected the hard-nosed Grady to go ballistic. He ignored Bryan and the other three players who'd been on the floor, walking past them to meet Joey.

Leaning his head close to the boy, he put his arm around him and said something meant for Joey's ears alone. Keri got a glimpse of Grady's face when he let Joey go and saw not anger, but determination.

He directed the five players who'd play the last five seconds to sit down so they could go over the strategy for the last play. Joey Jividen was one of the five.

"You've got to be kidding me," the man behind her groused loudly, while on the sidelines Grady pointed to his clipboard. Murmurs went up from the rest of the crowd.

"He needs to bench Joey," Carolyn said. "That boy's gonna lose us the game."

That boy, Keri thought, had just gotten a much-needed boost of confidence from his coach.

"I think Coach Quinlan's doing the right thing," Keri said.

"Bryan will take the last shot," Lori predicted. "The best player always does."

Everybody in the gym, including the opposing team, seemed to arrive at the same conclusion. Two Westlake defenders shadowed Bryan, clearly having been directed not to let him catch the pass.

Joey Jividen was the inbounder. He threw the ball not to Bryan, but to Lori's son Garrett. Because the defender who should have been assigned to Joey was double-teaming Bryan, Joey had an unimpeded lane to the basket.

Garrett passed Joey the basketball at the same spot where Joey had just missed the shot. Joey caught it, arching the ball toward the basket and victory before time expired.

This time there was no doubt. The ball banked off the backboard and dropped straight through the hoop.

The crowd went wild, the Springhill players mobbing the boy who had gone from goat to hero in a matter of seconds. Keri joined in the cheers. Grady walked onto the court to where his joyous players congregated, but not to partake in the celebration. In an eye blink, he had the Springhill team lined up single file to shake the opponents' hands.

It was only when the winning Springhill players were leaving the floor that Keri saw Grady pat young Joey Jividen on the back.

CHAPTER FOUR

WITH A SIGH OF RESIGNATION, Grady snagged a couple of pepperoni pizzas from the freezer section of the Food Mart and added them to a grocery cart that already contained the half-dozen frozen dinners that looked most edible.

He didn't have the healthiest diet around, but considering his grab-and-go style it was a step up from eating at a fast-food restaurant.

Grady had come to the grocery store straight from Wednesday's basketball practice, which had begun directly after school. Later, at home, he'd heat one of the dinners while watching game film of Springhill's next opponent.

He was busier on game days, and he preferred it that way. The whole coaching life suited him. It always had, which was why it had hurt so much to leave Carolina State. Leave? That was a mild word for it. He'd practically been chased out of town.

Shoving the thought from his mind, he steered his cart around the heavy freezers that showcased bags of mixed vegetables and packaged breakfast foods, then turned the corner. The same tall, thin girl he'd seen a few nights ago with Keri Cassidy stood in front of the ice cream, her slender index finger tapping her chin.

"Get the double chocolate fudge," Grady said.

She took a step backward, a guarded expression on a young face that reminded him of Bryan's. Same general shape, same big dark eyes, same olive complexion. Her hair was brown, too, but a few shades lighter than her brother's.

"You're Bryan Charleton's sister, right?"

She nodded. Her shoulders were slightly stooped, her posture a far cry from the way her self-assured brother carried himself. Bryan always looked him straight in the eye; his sister didn't lift her chin.

"I'm Coach Quinlan, Bryan's basketball coach," he said.

A hint of recognition crossed her face, followed by more silence.

"What's your name?" he prompted.

"Rose," she replied, the name barely audible.

He smiled, hoping to put her at ease. "So you gonna get the double chocolate fudge? It's my favorite."

She mumbled something unintelligible, opened the freezer door, snatched a carton of French vanilla ice cream and hurried away. He could have chalked her up as another in the growing line of Springhill citizens who disapproved of his coaching methods, but he didn't think that was it.

Rose Charleton's behavior seemed to have more to do with her own demons than with his.

He continued shopping, searching for Keri down every long, well-lit aisle. Rose wasn't old enough to drive, and he seriously doubted Bryan would hang around with his younger sister.

"You're Coach Quinlan, aren't you?"

The middle-aged lady in the long black coat asking the question had dark circles under her eyes and deep lines bracketing her mouth. She looked sad—and unfamiliar.

"That's right," Grady said.

"I'm Ruth Cartwright, Fuzz's wife."

He called up an image of her husband from the photographs hanging in his office. A broad-shouldered dynamo of a man with white hair short enough to earn him his nickname. Fuzz had been synonymous with Springhill basketball for as long as most people could remember. Grady would have shaken his wife's hand, but she kept a firm grip on the shopping cart handle.

"How is Mr. Cartwright?" Grady asked. The last he'd heard, Fuzz was recovering from quadruple bypass surgery.

"Impatient to get home," she said. "Angry that he can't coach."

"The boys miss him." Grady spoke the truth. If he polled his players on whether they wanted their old coach back, the vote would be unanimous. It wouldn't be in Grady's favor.

"He misses the boys, especially Bryan Charleton." Ruth Cartwright's tired eyes focused on him and came alive. "Fuzz says Bryan's good enough to lead the team to a state championship. He says you need to keep Bryan on court."

Frustration tugged at Grady, but he fought to keep his expression neutral. "It was nice seeing you, Mrs. Cartwright. You be sure to tell your husband I'm wishing him well."

Retreat seemed a better option than explaining that Bryan Charleton needed suspending, no matter that Becky

Harding had retracted her story. Becky had lied to Grady, but in his opinion it hadn't been when she claimed to be the author of Bryan's paper.

His grumbling stomach alerting him it was time for dinner, he groaned inwardly at the human logjam at the checkout counters. Until he noticed Keri Cassidy at the rear of one of the lines.

She stiffened enough for him to realize she'd seen him. Although one of the other lines was slightly shorter, he pulled his cart directly behind hers. "Hello, Ms. Cassidy."

Only her head turned, affording him a view of her profile and the graceful curve of her neck. She gave him a cursory, closemouthed smile. "Hello."

She faced forward, as though that was all she meant to say.

"I ran into Bryan's sister by the ice cream," he said. "How old is she? Thirteen? Fourteen?"

This time she turned to face him fully. Again she was dressed like she'd come from work, in brown slacks and the same brown coat he'd seen her wearing before. Her hair tumbled to her shoulders, as though the January wind had gotten hold of it and she hadn't yet smoothed it back in place. He found the disarray charming. "Fourteen."

"Ninth grade, right?"

"Right."

Despite her one-word answers, he persisted, "Where is she?"

"In the car with her iPod."

The woman in line in front of Keri placed a red plastic bar on the conveyor belt to indicate where her order stopped and Keri's started. Keri began removing items from her cart. Fruits. Vegetables. Chicken breasts. Skim milk. And just about every other healthy food the grocery store stocked.

"Is Rose on any of the school sports teams?" he asked to the back of her head.

She sighed loudly enough for him to hear. "Why are you so interested?"

His curiosity extended past Rose to Keri. He'd learned she'd taken custody of Bryan and Rose after their mother died in a single-car accident, but aside from that knew next to nothing about her—except she was once engaged to his cousin.

"If one kid in the family's athletic, the other one usually is, too," he answered.

"Yeah, well, Rose isn't involved in sports."

"Too bad," he said, and meant it. "It might help her get over her shyness."

"How so?" she asked with the first real glimmer of interest she'd shown since he'd gotten behind her in line.

"Sports are great for building self-esteem," he explained. "I see kids come out of their shells all the time."

A shutter seemed to slam over her face. "It won't work for Rose."

She reached into her cart for a box of low-fat crackers and laid it on the conveyor belt, dismissing him. Again.

"Why not?" he asked.

She pressed her lips together, then awarded him her full attention and said in a quiet voice, "Because she lost part of her leg in the accident that killed her mother. She wears a prosthesis."

Poor kid, he thought.

"There are prostheses designed especially for sports," he said in a voice as soft as hers. He should know. He'd taken a few classes in adapted physical education in college.

"That doesn't help Rose," she said. "Our insurance only pays for the basics, and I couldn't afford to buy something like that."

His mind whirled, thinking back to the instructor who'd taught the adapted PE course at Carolina State. It seemed to him that Ethan Everson—yes, that was his name—had a company that had something to do with prosthetic design. If he explained the situation, maybe Grady could get Mr. Everson to donate a prosthesis.

"What orthopedic practice does Rose use?" Grady asked.

Suspicion hovered over Keri, as visible as a cloud. "May and Gamble. Why?"

"Just curious," Grady said, reluctant to reveal the direction of his thoughts. He made it a practice never to promise something he couldn't deliver, and he wasn't even sure Ethan Everson would remember him. He almost snorted in derision. What was he thinking? Everybody at Carolina State would remember him.

"Ma'am, could you please put out some more groceries?" the cashier called.

"Oh. Sorry," Keri said, clearly not happy about holding up the line. She reached into her cart for a box of honey oat cereal at the same time Grady did. Their hands touched, and their eyes met. Awareness shimmered through him, but she pulled her hand away as if she'd been scorched.

"Thanks, but I can do it." She unloaded the rest of her groceries in a hurry, got out her wallet, swiped her debit card and punched in her access code. Within minutes, her groceries were bagged and paid for.

"I'll be right back," the cashier told Grady, then went off to help another cashier change a register tape.

Instead of leaving the store at high speed like he expected her to, Keri lingered. "I've been wondering something. Why haven't you said anything to me about Becky Harding?"

Her standoffishness suddenly made sense. "Were you expecting an apology?" he asked.

"If you apologize to anyone, it should be to Bryan." She cocked her head. "Surely he deserves one."

"He's not getting an apology from me."

"Why not?"

"Because I still think Becky wrote his paper."

"That's ridiculous," she refuted. "Becky admitted she lied."

"Only after most of the kids at school gave her a hard time," he said. "The way I heard it, some of the other cheerleaders refused to talk to her."

He expected her to argue, but a pensive expression stole over her face. "If you didn't believe Becky, why lift Bryan's suspension?"

"I had to. Becky retracted her story."

The return of the cashier cut off the rest of their conversation. Keri nodded shortly at Grady, then wheeled away with her cart of groceries, but the set of her shoulders no longer seemed so rigid.

Grady had the impression Keri no longer knew what to believe, but he was pragmatic enough to realize he could be indulging in wishful thinking.

"GREAT GAME FRIDAY."

Bryan grinned and knocked fists with the short kid he recognized from his biology class. What was his name?

"Thanks, Dan," he said, the name of the boy quickly coming to mind. Dan smiled widely, as though Bryan had been the one who congratulated him.

"Dog, you were sick Friday night." Another boy Bryan didn't know very well yelled from across the hall. His name was Fred.

"Thanks, yo!" he yelled back.

A trio of girls, one as cute as the next, all of them giggling, made him feel like he was a rock star.

"Good game, Bryan," they said, sounding like one person.

He looked at each one in turn. Katelyn. Samantha. Victoria. "Thank you very much."

"What am I? Invisible?" Hubie groused, trudging along beside him down the school's main hallway. "I played the game, too."

"We couldn't have won without you, Hub," Bryan said. "You killed 'em on D."

"Yeah, but I hardly scored. You had, what, twenty-five? And the guy you were defending didn't have more than six."

His opponent had actually scored only four points. "Something like that," Bryan said.

Man, he loved this. Not as much as playing the game.

He'd do that in an empty gym in the middle of Siberia. But all this recognition felt good.

To think that after his mom died, he'd thought he'd never feel good again. Holding back the tears was so hard it had hurt to breathe. If he hadn't immersed himself in basketball, he couldn't have gotten through it.

He'd always miss his mom, but he'd learned he could be happy again. Now that last week's mess with Becky Harding was behind him, things were finally going his way. He felt as if nothing could stop him from playing basketball on scholarship in college.

Except maybe Coach Hard-Ass.

Hubie suddenly emitted a low whistle. "Who is that?"

Bryan followed his friend's gaze. A girl he'd never seen before was walking toward them on the opposite side of the hall. She had long, straight blond hair, fair skin and a face he'd love to photograph. The hem of her blue jeans skirt was way too modest, especially because she had killer legs.

Bryan veered away from Hubie, toward the girl. "Hel-lo there."

The girl stopped dead. It was either that or plow into him, either of which were okay with Bryan.

Her eyes were the color of the sky, and her eyebrows just a few shades darker than her blond hair. Mmm, she was pretty.

He gave her his most charming grin. "Haven't seen you around before."

"It's her first day."

Bryan had been so focused on the new girl, he hadn't realized someone was with her. He transferred his attention to a short girl with frizzy brown hair. She was a grade behind him, he thought, but she'd taken a turn doing the announcements earlier in the school year. Emily Delacorte. That was her name.

"Hey, Em. I didn't see you there. So who's your friend?"

"Jackie Fitzgibbons," Emily supplied. "Jackie, Bryan Charleton and Hubie Brown. They play for the basketball team."

"No joke," Jackie said. Everyone was silent, so she gestured to the Springhill High basketball sweatshirts they both wore. "Pretty hard to miss."

"Welcome to Springhill," Hubie said, sounding like somebody had appointed him to the student welcoming committee.

Bryan kept his eyes trained on Jackie. "Where'd you transfer from?"

"Peabody High. It's in Raleigh, North Carolina."

"Jackie's been all over the place," Emily supplied eagerly. "Her dad just got out of the military so her family's moved a lot. Like gypsies."

Bryan laughed at the description, wanting to know more about her wandering family.

"Hey, Charleton. Way to go."

"You're the man, Bryan."

Students passed them on the left and right, greeting him with the same effusiveness he'd enjoyed a moment ago. He acknowledged them all, even though he wanted only to focus on Jackie.

"Junior or senior?" he asked. An older woman would present a challenge, but he was up to it.

"Junior." Even better. She moved to get around him. "Excuse me. I don't want to be late for class."

"Oh, sure," he said, but took a step sideways, preventing her from leaving. He hadn't said what he had to say yet. He leaned toward her, bending to make up for the difference in their heights. She smelled feminine, like those scented soaps Keri and Rose used. "Give me your cell number. I've got basketball practice after school, but later I'll take you to a terrific frozen custard place."

He dug in his jeans pocket for his cell phone, getting ready to enter her number.

"Thanks, but no," Jackie said firmly.

No? It wasn't a word he heard very often, if at all.

"You don't like frozen custard?" he asked.

"I like it fine. I just don't much like basketball." She actually smiled at him, although just with her lips. "Nice meeting you, Bryan, Hubie."

She sidestepped him and continued down the hall, her hips swaying gently as she increased the distance between them.

"Well, what do you know," Hubie said with a chuckle. "Not every girl at Springhill High wants to date you, after all."

"Shut up, Hubie."

"Lighten up, guy," Hubie said. "Everybody else in this whole damn school worships the hall you walk down."

As if on cue, Naomi, the girl he'd taken to the Snowball dance, blew him a kiss. "Call me sometime," she encouraged, even though he'd told her he wasn't ready for an exclusive relationship.

"See?" Hubie said. "You don't need Jackie what's her name. Lots of other girls are into you."

The thing was that at the moment only one girl interested Bryan. A girl who probably thought she'd successfully brushed him off.

If she'd ever seen him play basketball, she'd know she hadn't succeeded at all. Bryan prided himself on never giving up. Jackie Fitzgibbons would discover that soon enough.

KERI CLUTCHED THE PHONE in her right hand so tightly her fingernails dug into her palm.

"You're sure Rose isn't in class?" she asked the secretary who'd phoned the newspaper office. "Maybe it's a mistake."

"No mistake. I have the list in front of me. Rose's name isn't here."

Keri gritted her teeth, trying to hold back the panic that had been trying to strangle her since she heard the secretary's voice. She'd been a parent long enough to know the drill. When you didn't leave a message on the absentee hotline, the school system followed up with a phone call.

Keri did a quick mental replay of the events of that morning. While Rose picked at her cereal, Keri kissed her goodbye on the top of her head. Bryan swept into the kitchen, his gym bag slung over his shoulder, saying he was getting some shooting practice in before school. Keri impressed upon Rose the bus wouldn't wait if she was late.

The bus. Of course. That had to be it.

"I had to come into work early this morning. Rose must have missed the bus," Keri told the school secretary in a much calmer voice.

"Then get her to school as soon as you can," the secretary said.

"Sure thing." Keri disconnected the call with a press of her index finger. She didn't bother to put down the phone, quickly dialing her home number.

Each successive ring that went unanswered sent fresh dread rushing through Keri.

"We're off somewhere doing something," Bryan's recorded voice announced when the answering machine picked up. "Leave us a message."

"Rosie. It's Keri." Keri sounded panicked even to her own ears. "Pick up if you're there."

Silence.

If Rose was neither at school nor home, where could she be? They lived in a residential neighborhood about a mile from town, certainly a walkable distance. But the wintry mix that had fallen on Springhill last night had turned to ice this morning. Rose, who was still self-conscious of her prosthetic leg, wouldn't have ventured outside.

Keri felt sweat break out on her brow and above her upper lip.

"Rosie," she said again, her tone pleading. "Please pick up."

More silence.

She pictured the stairs leading from the first floor to the second, remembered how much difficulty Rose had navigating them in the initial months after being fitted for the prosthesis.

She envisioned Rose losing her balance, Rose falling, Rose lying broken at the foot of the staircase.

Keri's vision turned black, the bright colors of the ad

on her computer screen seeming to mock her. Slamming the phone down, she leapt to her feet and grabbed her purse from the back of her chair.

"I need to go home," she told her friend Jill, who was walking back to her computer.

"Everything all right?"

"I don't know," Keri said, unwilling to waste time explaining. "I'll call you as soon as I do."

She skipped the elevator in favor of the stairs and in what seemed like seconds rushed through the parking lot to her car. The smooth sole of her shoe shot out from under her, and she went down hard, landing flat on her bottom.

She sat stunned for a moment, then slowly got to her feet, brushing dirt off the back of her coat. Then she was in her car, hardly noticing her scraped hands and torn panty hose as she drove too fast through the streets of Springhill.

She jerked the Volvo to a stop in the driveway, pushed open the car door and hurried up the sidewalk to the house, her hand shaking when she inserted the key into the lock.

"Please, God, let her be okay," she prayed aloud.

She entered the house to…nothing. No crumpled girl at the foot of the steps. No horror. No sound except a faint purring. Bella, the cat who'd come with the kids, slunk into the room and peered at her with his yellow eyes. Rose said her mom had dubbed the cat Bella because it meant *beautiful* in Italian. But the cat's midnight-black coat and furtive manner always made Keri think of Bela Lugosi, the Hungarian actor famous for playing Count Dracula.

Never a cat person, Keri had reached an uneasy truce with Bella. She fed him; he tolerated her.

"Where's Rosie?" she asked the cat, who of course

couldn't tell her. She was losing it. She cupped her mouth and yelled, "Rosie."

She searched the house in quick order, ending in the kitchen. Rose's cereal bowl from that morning sat on the counter, but there was no sign of Rose. Keri needed to accept that she and Bella were the only ones in the house.

"The school made a mistake," she murmured aloud. There could be no other explanation.

That's when she heard it. A soft sound that sounded like…a sneeze? But where had it come from? Bella appeared in the doorway, moving silently to the closet-size pantry. They kept the door closed to shut Bella out. The cat meowed and pawed at the door.

Keri shooed the cat away, then opened the door. The pantry was set up like a walk-in closet, with shelves on three sides of a narrow entryway. Rose sat with her back resting against the rear shelf, hugging her knees.

"Rosie!" Keri lowered herself beside the girl, gathering her close and hugging her tight. She breathed in the scent of soap and strawberry-scented shampoo. "I was so worried about you."

"I'm fine," Rose said in a small voice.

Rose was fine. Now that worry no longer interfered with her power of reason, Keri could think again. She drew back and searched the teenager's guilt-ridden face.

"Were you hiding from me?" she asked.

Rose's huge green eyes grew sad.

"You *were* hiding from me. You heard me on the phone, too. But you didn't want me to know you were home." Keri scooted backward, putting some distance between them so she could see Rose more clearly. "Why aren't you in school?"

"I missed the bus," she said.

"On purpose or by mistake? Tell the truth."

"On purpose."

"Get up," Keri said in a harsh voice she hardly recognized as her own. "I'm taking you to school."

"But Keri—"

"No buts. Get your backpack and your books. I'm so mad at you right now that I suggest you keep your mouth shut."

They completed the trip to the high school in silence broken only by the sound of Rose's sniffling. The pitiful sound tugged at Keri's heart, but she wouldn't let it sway her. Instead of dropping Rose off in front of the school like she usually did, Keri swung into the visitor's lot.

"You don't have to walk me in," Rose said.

"If I want to make sure you get there, I do," Keri told her.

Rose shot her a hurt look, then got out of the car. Keri had spent the drive trying to decide on a suitable punishment. Rose hardly left the house so grounding wouldn't work. Neither did it make sense to ban reading, her favorite pastime.

"No television for two weeks," she said when they were inside the school.

Rose walked in front of her to the office, resentment evident in every step. Even through her anger, Keri realized Rose had turned a corner in her recovery. When Rose first learned to use the prosthesis, she swayed when she walked. Sometimes, when she was tired, she still limped. But not now.

Rose stood sullenly beside her when they checked in at the front desk, saying nothing.

"I'll have to put her tardiness down as unexcused," the secretary said.

"It won't happen again." Keri slanted Rose a meaningful glance.

Keri caught the sheen of tears in Rose's eyes before the girl stalked off. Her anger spent, despair washed over Keri. She longed to call Rose back, hug her tight and take back the punishment. But she couldn't. Not if Rose was to learn there were consequences for her actions.

Blindly, Keri pushed open the office door and heard a thud. Through the clear glass, she saw a man rubbing his arm. Not just any man. Grady Quinlan. He moved away from the door. Inwardly groaning, she stepped into the hall. He wore a Springhill basketball T-shirt tucked into low-slung navy sweatpants, standard wear for a PE teacher. The definition in his arms and the flatness of his stomach weren't standard.

"Sorry," she said. "I didn't see you."

His hazel eyes cut to the door.

"I was upset." She stopped abruptly, not sure why she'd told him that.

"Upset about what?" His eyes moved over her, and she belatedly acknowledged she must look a fright in her dirt-stained coat and ripped panty hose. Why hadn't she thought to change before leaving the house? Because she'd been angry, she answered herself.

"It doesn't matter," she said vaguely.

"Sure it does." He focused on her as though genuinely interested in her problem, reaching some need deep inside her.

"Rose skipped school today," she blurted out. "I didn't find out about it until the office called."

That laser-focus didn't waver. "Why?"

"Because I didn't call her in sick."

"Not why did the office call. Why did Rose skip school?"

"Because…" Her voice trailed off as she realized he'd asked a question she hadn't. She swallowed. "I didn't ask her."

"You still can."

Stated that way, it sounded so simple, but nothing about raising two teenagers was easy.

"I don't care what her excuse is, she shouldn't have skipped," Keri said defensively.

"No, she shouldn't have," he agreed.

She tried to find something in his response at which to take offense but couldn't. "Do you have children, Mr. Quinlan?"

"Call me Grady," he said easily. "And no. No children. No wife, either."

She filed his unmarried status away, a part of her glad to have it confirmed, another part of her annoyed that she was glad. "Then what makes you an expert?"

He put up his hands. "I'm no expert. I teach, remember? I know a lot of this stuff is hit and miss."

Keri immediately felt ashamed. He'd been trying to help her, and she'd snapped at him.

"Thanks for the suggestion," she told him.

He smiled, softening the too-serious lines around his mouth, lighting up his eyes and bringing Keri to a conclusion she must have known on some level all along. Grady Quinlan was hot.

"Anytime," he said.

She nodded and moved past him. The feeling that swept through her was ridiculous, but for the first time in a very long time she didn't feel so alone.

CHAPTER FIVE

GRADY'S FIRST CHOICE of a place to meet his cousin Tony for a drink Saturday night wouldn't have been the Springhill Bowlarama. He wouldn't have elected to meet his cousin at all, but Mary Lynn hadn't given him much choice.

After Springhill had won last night's basketball game by a wide margin, Mary Lynn approached him full of congratulations and good news.

"I'm an aunt," she'd crowed. "My sister Renee had her baby this morning. A little boy named Chad. Seven pounds, four ounces."

"That's great!" Grady, his spirits high from Springhill's big win, was easily charmed by her enthusiasm. As well as sympathetic at the tears that sprang to her eyes.

"I'm sorry," Mary Lynn said, swiping them away. "It's just that Tony and I haven't been so lucky."

"Mary Lynn…" Tony had appeared behind his wife, a warning tone in his voice Grady interpreted to mean he wanted her to keep quiet.

"Anyway, our mom's on a cruise so I'm leaving tomorrow morning to help Renee when she gets home from the hospital," Mary Lynn had continued. "I'll be back Sunday night, but I hate to think of Tony all alone."

Tony thrust out a hand for Grady to shake, unsuccessfully trying to turn the topic back to basketball and Bryan Charleton's thirty-point night.

"I was just telling Grady how much I didn't want you to spend the weekend alone." Mary Lynn laid a hand on her husband's arm.

"I'll be fine." Tony sounded irritated. "I'll probably just do some work around the house, maybe go out for a drink Saturday night."

"You'll go with him, right, Grady?" Mary Lynn asked.

And that's how Grady found himself agreeing to meet his cousin at the Bowlarama Bar. He ordered a draft beer from the bartender, then settled at a table with a view of the lanes to wait for Tony.

He supposed getting out of the house on a Saturday night wasn't a bad thing. He'd been alone too much since leaving Carolina State, first on the open road in his eighteen-wheeler and now cooped up in his duplex watching basketball. College games, pro games, game film. You name it, he watched it.

Nothing dictated that he needed to stay at the Bowlarama Bar for long. He'd have one drink, two at the most, then head on home. Maybe he'd talk to somebody besides Tony before he left. Maybe not.

His gaze strayed to the group of boisterous women on some nearby lanes giving one another high fives. A bank of glass separated the bar from the lanes, making them seem like actors in a silent movie.

He supposed he could try to meet some women, but his heart wasn't in it. He sometimes wondered how he'd gotten to the age of twenty-seven without a single serious long-term relationship. He supposed the answer had to do with basketball, which had long served as the love of his life. Since leaving Carolina State he'd had exactly two dates—with two women who'd asked him out, then asked too many questions.

The only woman who'd interested him in a very long time was Keri Cas—

The unmistakable proud shoulders caught his eye. He sat up straighter, leaning closer to the glass panel. Yes, the woman in the slim black jeans and striped long-sleeved shirt was Keri. She took a few steps toward the lane, brought the heavy bowling ball to her waist, then went into a backswing, releasing the ball in front of her.

It wobbled down the edge of the lane before dropping into the gutter.

She turned, tossing back her hair and laughing. The laughter lit up her face, rendering it not merely attractive but beautiful. And young. So young. He'd never seen her without worry etching her features.

"Hey, R.G." Tony sat down beside him.

Grady started, surprised he hadn't noticed his cousin enter the bar. Before saying another word, Tony very deliberately scanned the lanes beyond the glass. His gaze stopped on the same lane that had interested Grady.

And Grady now knew why Tony had suggested they meet at the bar attached to the bowling alley.

"You knew Keri Cassidy would be bowling," he said.

Tony's laugh rang false. "That's a strange thing to say."

"Not so strange," Grady commented. "Mary Lynn said you two used to be engaged."

Tony's face instantly sobered. "Mary Lynn talks too much. Why would she tell you that, anyway?"

Grady took a long pull of beer, putting the pieces of the puzzle together as he swallowed. Tony's furtive conversation with Keri in the hall. Mary Lynn's insistence that Grady join Tony for a drink. Tony's suggestion they meet at the Bowlarama.

"Maybe Mary Lynn's afraid you're trying to start something up again," he said.

"That's bull," Tony said quickly.

"So you didn't know Keri would be here?"

Tony massaged the back of his neck. "Okay. Yeah. I knew. A buddy of mine is married to a friend of hers. He mentioned Keri was filling in on his wife's bowling team tonight."

Grady only cocked an eyebrow. He didn't need to point out to Tony that Tony was married.

"It's not what you think," Tony said. "Keri and me, we used to be...close. Now we don't even talk. I just want us to be friends again."

Grady nodded toward the entrance to the bar that led from the bowling alley. Keri must have thrown the gutter ball on the last frame because she followed three women into the bar. "Your friend is here."

Tony pointed to a large wooden table nearby that seated eight. "Grab that table, and I'll see if they want to join us."

Without waiting for Grady to agree, Tony approached Keri's foursome. The women hadn't seen Tony yet, but Grady could guess how his cousin would proceed. He'd direct his invitation to his buddy's wife, then Keri would be well and truly stuck.

"CAN'T YOU JUST TAKE ME home first?" Keri asked Jill before her friend could signal for the bartender. "It's getting late. I don't want to leave Rose home alone for much longer."

"It's barely past nine," Jill said, relying on the two other women who'd made up their bowling team to attract the bartender's attention. "And you've already called Rose twice. Trust me, she's fine."

Keri knew that was probably true, but Rose already spent too much time alone as it was. In fact, it was one of the reasons Keri seldom went out. Being a normal teenage boy, Bryan wasn't often interested in keeping his sister company. When he wasn't playing basketball, he was off with his friends.

Keri fidgeted. Even though she'd had a good time tonight, she was starting to regret letting Jill talk her into filling in for a vacationing team member.

"Stop worrying," Jill ordered. "If you still want to go home after one drink, I'll take you. But this is part of our routine. We bowl for beers."

"The high scorer doesn't pay," interjected Lucy Smith, a redhead dressed in pink who'd had an impressive string of strikes. She giggled. "The high scorer doesn't drive home, either."

"Well, what do you know? Jill and Keri."

Keri recognized the voice before the man sidled up next to them. Tony Marco wore a wide smile on a face she'd once thought so handsome she'd go weak in the knees at the sight of him. That seemed a very long time ago.

"Two of my favorite people to run into," Tony continued.

Keri didn't smile back. She felt as though she and Tony

had been playing a game of dodgeball, with Keri being the one trying to avoid the ball. Since Tony's previous pattern had been to avoid her whenever possible, she wasn't sure why he'd suddenly started seeking her out. But she didn't believe for a second this meeting was coincidental, not when he'd left three messages on her answering machine in as many weeks imploring her to call him.

"Tony, great to see you," Jill said. Jill had shared recently that her husband and Tony played at the same golf club. That connection was probably how Tony knew Keri would be at the bowling alley tonight. "Are you here with Mary Lynn?"

Tony had the grace to look guilty, if only for a second. "Nope. She's out of town." He gestured toward a large table in the middle of the bar. "I'm with my cousin."

Keri's eyes swung to the table, locking with Grady Quinlan's. Energy crackled between them, as if on a thick, invisible cable. A corner of his mouth lifted slightly, softening the square jaw that sometimes made him appear obstinate. He lifted a beer mug in acknowledgment.

"Cute cousin," Jill said. "We'd love to join you. Wouldn't we, ladies?"

Lucy Smith and Anne Jablonski, the other member of the bowling team, readily agreed. Even if Keri wanted to object, she was outnumbered. Although she privately admitted the prospect of a drink didn't seem as unattractive as it had a few minutes ago.

Tony insisted on paying for the pitcher of beer the group had ordered. Keri grabbed one of the frosted mugs from the bar, then accompanied the other ladies to the table. Jill sat down first, two seats down from Grady.

Quickly sizing up the situation, Keri realized she could avoid sitting next to Tony if she claimed the empty seat between Jill and Grady. She hurried to take it.

Grady didn't get up but pulled out the chair for her. He wore khaki pants and a stone-colored canvas shirt, a color that went well with his coloring. She noticed his hands were broad with long fingers, hands probably equally adept palming a basketball or stroking a woman.

Keri paused for a moment, confused. She wasn't looking to start up anything with Bryan's coach. Or with anybody else.

"Hi, Keri." His use of her given name, spoken in that low voice of his, seemed intimate.

"Hello," she said formally, sounding distressingly like her mother.

She snuck a peek at him. Even sitting down, he looked like an athlete. The perception had as much to do with his carriage as the width of his shoulders and his short haircut. Some women might find the black-haired, black-eyed Tony more striking, but Keri thought Grady projected a quiet dignity that was far more attractive.

The next few minutes passed in a whirl of introductions and laughter. Keri waited until everybody else had poured from the pitcher, then filled her mug halfway.

"Is that all you're having?" Jill sounded incredulous.

"I'm not much of a drinker," Keri said. An understatement. Since taking custody of Bryan and Rose, she didn't drink at all. The last time she'd been in a bar, she'd been engaged to Tony.

"Nothing wrong with that," Grady said. "I don't drink much myself."

She slanted him a grateful smile.

"Keri prefers wine." Tony half rose. "I'll get you a glass."

"No." Keri's response came out sharper than she would have liked. "I mean, no, thanks. I'm not staying long."

She checked her watch. Nine-thirty. She wondered what Rose was doing.

"The deal was one drink," Jill reminded her.

"What deal?" Grady asked so only she could hear.

She responded just as softly. "Jill said she wouldn't drive me home until I had a drink."

"You want to go home?"

She thought of Rose. "More than anything."

"Take a sip," he told her.

Puzzled, she complied, the bitter taste of the beer reminding her why she'd never gotten in the habit of drinking the stuff.

"Okay," Grady said, "now I'll take you home."

"But I couldn't ask you to go to the trouble."

"No trouble. I'm ready to leave, anyway. So do you want that ride?"

She made a snap decision. "Yes."

He dug out his wallet, threw a few bills on the table and stood up. "I'm driving Keri home."

Jill seemed about to protest, but then her mouth snapped shut and curved into a smile. Approval practically oozed from her, but now wasn't the time for Keri to tell her friend she'd jumped to the wrong conclusion.

"You're what?" Tony shook his head and put both hands on the table, ready to push himself up. "No, you stay here. I'll drive Keri home."

"I already offered." Grady projected an air of being in charge, the same way he did on the basketball court with his players. "Let's go, Keri."

Half afraid Tony would follow them into the night, Keri didn't stop looking over her shoulder until she was ensconced in Grady's silver Toyota MR2.

"Thanks," she told him as he pulled out of the parking lot.

"You're welcome."

She relaxed against the back of the passenger seat, one of only two seats in the car, and breathed in the smell of leather. "Your car's nice. But as tall as you are, I would have expected you to drive something bigger."

"I got a great deal on it used. After driving the eighteen-wheeler, I needed a change."

"You drove a truck? When?"

"Before I came to Springhill."

"Why would—"

"I need your street address," he said. "Specific directions would help unless you're in the mood to drive around town. I'm still pretty new here."

She provided her address, curious as to why he'd changed the subject. And why somebody with a teaching degree had been driving a truck.

Her house was in a modest residential neighborhood not more than two miles from the bowling alley. In what seemed like no time, he pulled into her driveway and shut off the ignition. Rose had once again forgotten to turn on the porch light, but Keri vowed not to make a big deal about it. After the way she'd handled Rose skipping school, she needed to lighten up.

"I'll walk you to the door," Grady said, preparing to get out of the car.

"Wait." Keri laid a hand on Grady's forearm, which felt strong and solid under his brown leather jacket. "I need to tell you something."

Only his head moved when he turned to her. The rest of him was perfectly still. The car was almost entirely in darkness except for a faint glow from the moon. It didn't cast enough light for her to see more than the outline of his features. The strong chin. The bold slope of his nose. The sensual softness of his mouth.

She moved her hand from his arm, placing it in her lap. "You were right about Rose. I should have asked why she cut school before I jumped down her throat."

"Why did she cut?"

"They were choosing lab partners in biology. She was afraid she wouldn't get picked," Keri explained, relating Rose's reason, which the girl hadn't shared until hours after Keri asked for an explanation. It had been at bedtime, after Rose turned off the light, and Keri had stuck her head in the bedroom to say she loved her. She'd heard tears in Rose's voice.

"I thought it might be something like that," Grady said.

"How? I live with her, and I didn't pick up on it."

She heard the brush of leather on leather when he shrugged. "I know kids. Rose is the kind who keeps to herself."

"Too much to herself," Keri said. "I'm always suggesting she call a friend, but I'm not sure she has anybody to call."

"Have you had her talk to somebody?"

"You mean a psychologist? She saw one pretty regularly after the accident, but about a year ago said she was through. I can't even get her to go to the school guidance counselor now."

"Then why do *you* think she has problems making friends?"

"I'm not sure. Maybe because of her leg. She can't do some of the things the other kids can."

He shook his head. "It's not because of how other people look at her. It's because of how she looks at herself."

"You mean she thinks of herself as less than whole?"

"Exactly."

Keri bit her lip, thinking over what he'd said. It made a lot of sense. Maybe Keri herself had even added to Rose's problems by allowing her to avoid trying new things. She swiped a hand over her face. "Sometimes I feel like I don't know what the hell I'm doing."

She recognized her mistake almost as soon as the words left her mouth. "I shouldn't have said that," she said quickly. "Especially to you."

"Why especially to me?" He leaned closer to her. He smelled clean and masculine.

"You'll think I don't know how to handle Bryan. But that's not true. Bryan never gives me any trouble. He's a very good kid. I wish I could make you see that."

His eyes didn't leave her face. "I see a woman two kids are very lucky to have in their lives," he said softly.

He touched her cheek, and her heart thudded. She was struck with how alone they were. The interior of the car created a cocoon containing just the two of them, their warm breath already starting to fog the windows. The scent of leather mixed with the heady smell of warm skin and man.

He moved imperceptibly toward her. He was going to kiss her, she thought, and she was going to let him.

She heard the intake of his breath, followed by a tapping that seemed out of place. It took her a few seconds to notice it came from the car window. She sprang away from him.

Grady calmly pushed the button that rolled down the window. Keri couldn't see who stood in the driveway but recognized Bryan's voice immediately.

"This is a private drive...." A beat of silence, followed by, "Coach Quinlan. What are you doing here?"

"Hello, Bryan," Grady said as though he'd run across the boy in the hall at school. "I'm talking to Keri."

Bryan's face filled the open window. He gaped at her in what looked like horror. Keri realized how the situation must appear.

"Your coach drove me home from the bar," Keri said, then could have kicked herself. "I mean, from bowling. I told you. I filled in on Jill's team tonight."

"Whatever." Bryan straightened from the window and sauntered into the house without a backward glance.

"I should go talk to him." Keri opened the door, feeling the rush of cold air over her heated cheeks. "I think he got the wrong impression."

Grady nodded, his hands on the steering wheel as though he didn't trust them anywhere near her. Despite Bryan's attitude, she found herself reluctant to leave.

"Thanks," she said. "Not just for the ride, but for talking to me about Rose."

"Anytime," he said.

She looked at her house, then turned back to Grady. "I'm not looking forward to this. Bryan won't understand."

"Or maybe he will," offered Grady.

Later, after Keri insisted to a sullen Bryan that nothing was going on between her and his coach, she replayed Grady's comment and figured out she could take it two ways.

What had he meant? That he thought nothing was going on between the two of them? Or that something was?

THE MESSAGE ON KERI'S answering machine didn't make sense.

Correction. The *messages* didn't compute, but she wasn't up to deciphering the meaning of yet another call from Tony Marco. She didn't even listen to Tony's messages the entire way through anymore.

Why would May and Gamble Orthopedics call to ask her to schedule an appointment so Rose could be fitted for a new prosthesis?

With the exception of Wednesdays, when Keri stayed late at the office, Keri worked weekdays from eight to four-thirty so she could be home when Rose was home. A quick glance at her kitchen wall clock showed it wasn't yet five, a good bet that the orthopedic office was still open.

She quickly dialed the number, which she knew by heart, and explained to the receptionist, whom she knew by name, that the prosthesis Rose had now fit well. "It doesn't make sense, Darla. The last time we were there, Dr. May said this prosthesis should last for a while unless Rose starts growing again."

"Let's see," Darla began, and Keri heard the rustle of papers. "Here. This explains it. The new prosthesis won't replace her existing one, it'll only be worn for sports or when she's exercising."

"For sports? That can't be right. I've checked with your office before about a sports prosthesis. Our insurance won't pay for it."

"So you didn't arrange this?" Darla asked.

"I don't know anything about it."

"Let me put you on hold, and I'll check Rose's chart."

The singing voice of somebody who may have been a former *American Idol* contestant drifted over the phone line. Keri blotted it out, trying to remember whom she'd talked to recently about a special prosthesis. Darla clicked back on before she came up with an answer.

"It says here that Everson Prosthetics is providing the prosthesis at no cost to you," Darla said.

"I've never heard of Everson Prosthetics."

"I can understand you wanting to get to the bottom of this, but why not go ahead and make the appointment? Sounds to me like it's a wonderful opportunity for Rose."

Darla was right. The prosthesis would enable Rose to lead a more active life, opening up a whole world Keri feared had been lost to her. But Keri couldn't help thinking there was a catch.

"Does it also mention someone teaching Rose how to use the prosthesis?" she asked. "If insurance won't pay for the prosthesis, I doubt it'll pay for a physical therapist."

"I'll have to—" Darla stopped, further deflating the balloon of hope that had started to rise in Keri. "Wait a minute. I see a notation here that somebody's volunteered to work with Rose after the initial fitting."

"Who?"

"Grady Quinlan. Does that name ring a bell?"

The bell rang so loudly and insistently that after Keri hung up she had to force herself not to drive to the Springhill High gym and find out what was going on.

Bryan wouldn't appreciate her showing up at basketball practice to talk to Grady. After Saturday night, he'd probably conclude the two of them were conducting a secret affair. That was the outcome for which her friend and coworker Jill was rooting.

Keri quashed the thought of what it would be like to make love to Grady before it could form, concentrating instead on her dilemma. It would be best to wait until tonight and talk to Grady over the phone.

Except Grady wasn't listed in the phone book because of his recent move to Springhill, and Directory Assistance claimed not to have a listing for a Grady Quinlan.

With the exception of Tony Marco, whom she refused to contact, the only person she could think of who'd have Grady's phone number was Bryan.

"I'm glad you were home in time for dinner," she told Bryan later that evening after Rose went upstairs to take a shower. He didn't join them often. The boys' and girls' basketball teams shared gym space and juggled practice times. If the boys' team had either the late practice slot or a game, Keri wouldn't have had the chance to talk to him.

"Me, too." Bryan paused in the act of rinsing dirty plates to grin at her. "I love your chicken tacos."

She rolled up some leftover chicken and shredded cheddar cheese in a whole-wheat taco shell. From experience, she knew leftovers in a house where a teenage boy lived never went to waste.

"That's the first time you've smiled all night," she said.

He turned back to the sink. "Not much to smile about."

She frowned. "Something happen at practice?"

"The usual," Bryan said. "Coach running us to death because he can."

"Isn't running what basketball players do?"

"Well, yeah. But you think he'd cut us a break after we won the last game by thirty."

She remembered the practice she'd watched, where Grady insisted every player touch every line. "Sounds like he's trying to make you guys the best you can be."

His gaze was as cutting as a laser. "You on his side now?"

She pursed her lips. "I didn't realize there were sides."

The plates he bent down to put in the dishwasher clanked against the other dishes. "He's not a good guy, okay?"

"You might change your mind after you hear this." She took a deep breath, feeling silly for being nervous about sharing news with Bryan. This was Bryan. They talked about everything. "A prosthetic company is donating a sports prosthesis for Rose."

Bryan's smile was instant. "That's great. Maybe she can run track again."

"Again?" Keri asked. "Rose ran track before?"

"When she was in grade school. She was really fast so Mom signed her up for this track team for little kids. That was the summer before…" His voice trailed off. "Anyway, Rose loved it."

"Why didn't I know this?"

"Guess there was no point talking about it after the accident." He picked up another dirty plate to rinse. "But I don't get it. What does Coach Quinlan have to do with this?"

"I think he got the company to donate the prosthesis."

"What?" Water streamed over the plate Bryan held under the tap.

"He supposedly offered to teach her how to use it."

Bryan's eyes turned to dark, fathomless slits. "What do you mean by supposedly?"

"That's what the secretary from the orthopedist's office said. But I haven't asked Grady about it yet." Keri opened the refrigerator and put the leftover tacos on the middle shelf. "I was hoping you had his phone number."

"You're going to call him?"

"How else can I find out what's going on?"

"Isn't it obvious?" He sounded incredulous. "He's not going to all this trouble because he's such a good guy. He's trying to get with you so he can ruin my life."

Keri suppressed a sigh. "That's a terrible thing to say. And why would he want to ruin your life, anyway?"

"Because he can. I already told you, he's on a power trip."

Bryan's argument didn't make any more sense now than it had before. "This is about Rose, not you. Or me."

"He's got you snowed if you believe that."

"I still need his phone number."

Bryan shut off the tap, put the last plate in the dishwasher and dug his cell phone from the gym bag he'd left on the floor by the door. He clicked some numbers, then read off his coach's number in brusque tones.

She hunted down a piece of scrap paper and was still writing down the last of the digits when he left the kitchen.

"That didn't go well," she muttered to herself, but then she hadn't expected it to.

She could still hear Rose's shower running upstairs so figured there wouldn't be a better time to call Grady. She listened to the phone ring five times, concluded he wasn't home and was hanging up when she heard his hello.

She brought the phone back up to her ear. "Oh, um, I hope I'm not interrupting anything."

"Who is this?"

She closed her eyes, feeling her cheeks flush, exceedingly glad he couldn't see her. "I'm sorry. It's Keri."

When he didn't respond, she added, "Cassidy. Keri Cassidy."

He laughed, the sound low and sexy. "I know who you are. I was just about to call you."

"You were?"

"As soon as I finished watching this game film. I didn't want to interrupt your dinner."

"We're done eating," she said.

"So how are things going with Rose?"

His question transported her back to the intimate conversation they'd shared in his car. She could see the night closing around them, hear her heart beat faster when he'd leaned toward her, almost feel the imprint of his mouth on hers. She cleared the images from her mind.

"Better," she said. "Is that why you were going to call? To ask about Rose?"

"You could say that," he answered.

She cleared her throat, annoyed at herself. Since taking custody of the kids, she couldn't afford to get flustered.

"Actually, Rose is the reason I'm calling," she said. "Her orthopedist said you arranged to have an Everson Prosthetics get her a sports prosthesis."

He groaned. "They already set it up? I'm sorry, Keri. I didn't know it would happen so fast. I wanted to be the one to tell you."

"You mean it's true?" Despite all the evidence, she could barely process the news.

"A former professor of mine designs prostheses. I gave him a call, and he came through. The insurance stuff can get tricky so that's why I volunteered to work with Rose."

"Wow," she said. "That's an incredible offer."

"Talk it over with Rose," he said. "After she gets fitted for the prosthesis, we can set up a time to get together."

"But—" She didn't finish her thought.

"I took adapted PE in college, if that's what you're worried about."

"It's not that. I'm just wondering why you're doing this," she said, then could have kicked herself. The next thing she knew, she'd be asking if Grady really was trying to get with her to ruin Bryan's life.

"I want to help her," he said simply.

"But why go to these lengths?"

"Why adopt two kids when you're in your early twenties and unmarried?" he countered.

"I get your point," she said softly.

"Good. Then I'll see you soon?"

"Yes," she said, already feeling like it wouldn't be soon enough.

CHAPTER SIX

BRYAN ADJUSTED HIS DRESS slacks before settling into his habitual seat at the very rear of the Spanish class. He tugged at his collar, then loosened the knot of the tie he'd gotten Keri to fix for him that morning.

He couldn't stay mad at Keri, not when it wasn't her fault that Coach Hard-Ass was worming his way into her life. How could Bryan blame Keri for being excited about that damn sports prosthesis when he was, too?

He'd half expected Rose to veto the idea, but she surprised him by saying she'd give it a try. His sister had been willing to try so few things since the accident that this was big.

Too bad somebody besides Coach hadn't arranged it.

Señor Myers, which is what the Spanish teacher insisted the students call him, said something that probably translated to "Take your seats."

Bryan leaned back and stretched his long legs in front of him, his eyes drifting to half-mast. He'd stayed up late instant-messaging with friends after everyone else had gone to sleep last night. Maybe he could sneak in some shut-eye before tonight's game.

Señor Myers droned on in Spanish, with Bryan understanding about every third word until the teacher said the name Jackie Fitzgibbons.

Bryan's eyes flashed all the way open.

The new girl stood next to the teacher, a smile curving her gorgeous lips, her blond hair straight and shiny. She wore another of those too-long skirts and a scoop-necked top that covered absolutely everything.

He hadn't talked to her since she shot him down, but whenever he saw her he held up his cell phone and quirked a questioning eyebrow. The last two or three times, he'd even coaxed a smile out of her.

He concentrated on the Spanish, wishing he understood better but guessing Jackie had transferred into Spanish Two because the Spanish One class wasn't challenging enough.

The boy who usually sat next to him was absent with the flu, leaving the seat next to him vacant.

Bryan stopped slouching, suddenly very glad team policy required players to dress up for away games. He couldn't look better than he did right now.

After Señor Myers dismissed her, Jackie headed for the empty seat. Her step faltered when her eyes fell on him, but she didn't have much choice about where to sit. Stray backpacks were piled over the only other available seat in the room.

"*Hola, chica lindo,*" he drawled.

"*Chica linda,*" she corrected in a whisper.

Oh, yeah. The endings of Spanish nouns and adjectives had to agree. "I like a smart girl," he whispered back, adding a wink to tell her that wasn't all he liked.

Señor Myers directed a cool stare their way but didn't tell them to *silencio,* or whatever the word was. Bryan clamped his mouth shut. The *señor* could bore a log to death, but he was a good-enough guy.

Bryan watched Jackie instead of the teacher, enjoying the way she tucked her long hair behind her ear when she leaned over to write something down and the little lines that appeared between her brows when she concentrated. If he had his camera, he'd risk annoying Señor Myers by taking her picture.

Halfway through class, he ripped a corner from a piece of notebook paper and scribbled down his cell number. She wouldn't look at him so he made a sound to get her attention and held out the note. Her pretty blue eyes flashed a refusal, and she shook her head.

"*Por favor,*" he mouthed, the Spanish words for *please*.

She sighed, then checked to make sure Señor Myers was looking away before quickly snatching the note from him.

When she unfolded it, the corners of her mouth twitched.

Mine, he'd written before his cell number. After it, he'd put a simple question: *Yours?*

She stole another glance at the teacher, then wrote on the back of the note. Finally, he thought, barely stopping himself from pumping his fist in victory.

He took his time unfolding the note after she passed it to him, not wanting her to know how eager he was.

Give it up, it read.

He smiled through his frustration. He couldn't help himself.

He was gathering up his books after class, being quick about it so Jackie wouldn't slip away, when Keisha Collins approached wearing Springhill High sweats. The girls basketball team played at home when the boys were away, and the Lady Cougars typically dressed in matching team sweat suits.

"Hey, Bryan," Keisha said. "Reverend Martin wants to have a short meeting tomorrow night about the free throws."

"What time?"

"Eight," she said. "I told him we'd both be finished with practice by then."

"I'm there," he said.

The exchange didn't take long, but he was afraid Jackie had already left the room. He was surprised to find her still beside her desk, staring at him.

"Reverend Martin's the pastor at Grace Church," she said. "My family just joined."

Another chance to run into her. "Then we'll be going to the same church."

The prospect didn't appear to excite her. She cocked her head. "Why does the Reverend want to meet with you about your free throws?"

Bryan laughed. "Not *my* free throws. The free-throw contest we're holding for the kids after services in a couple weeks."

"We?"

"It was my idea. You know there's a Grace Elementary School, right? This will raise money for the school's athletic programs."

"You went to Grace School?"

"My sister did. They were so good to her after it happened that I wanted to give back."

"After what happened?"

He was so used to everybody in Springhill knowing his business he'd forgotten Jackie was new in town.

"Rose lost part of her leg in a car accident," he explained, finding it easier to omit what he and Rose both lost. "Afterward, the people at the church and the school were really nice to her."

"I'm sorry that happened to her." Jackie seemed to be searching his face, but he didn't know what she was looking for. "This contest? What age group does it involve?"

"Eight to twelve. Boys and girls."

"My brother's eight."

"Then he should come," Bryan said. "Give me your cell number and I'll call you with the details."

Jackie's eyes sparkled with amusement. "I'll hear about it on the church announcements."

"Okay, if you want to gamble," he said lightly. Out of the corner of his eye, he spotted Señor Myers alone in front of the room. "Don't go anywhere. I need to tell Señor something."

He said what he had to say as quickly as possible, then rejoined Jackie. They walked out of the classroom together.

"What was that all about?" she asked.

He shrugged. "Just telling Señor Myers I can't turn in my homework tomorrow."

Those blue eyes swung to his. "Why not?"

"We have a game tonight."

"So?"

"So I won't have time to do it."

Her eyebrows arched. "So if I had a concert tonight, he'd let me turn in my homework late, too?"

He frowned, wondering at the edge in her voice. "I don't know. Ask him."

"I wouldn't ask."

She was making less sense by the second. "Why not?"

"Because..." she began, then stopped. "Never mind. You wouldn't understand."

She picked up her pace, leaving him behind. He would have chased after her if a couple of his teammates hadn't converged on him, raising their fists to be bumped.

Jackie Fitzgibbons was right about one thing, Bryan thought, as he went through the motions of camaraderie.

He didn't understand what had just happened, at all.

GRADY ANCHORED ONE HAND on the rail at the front of the bus, counting heads and coming up one short. Damn. This was not a good night to leave a player behind in the opposing team's gym.

Valley View had been the cream of the AAA class for the past few years, a team so dominant in its district it scheduled tough nondistrict opponents for stiffer competition.

Grady had heard the Valley View coaches made sure no added opponent was good enough to threaten their team's undefeated record.

That hadn't worked out too well tonight.

Springhill was an AA school, with an enrollment about half the size of Valley View's. It had trailed the bigger, faster Valley View team for the entire game but pulled to within two points in the closing seconds.

The fans in the raucous student section had already been celebrating their victory when Bryan Charleton stole the ball and hit a desperation three-pointer at the buzzer for the Springhill win.

The gym had gone silent. Then came the inevitable cries that time had expired before the shot. The referees ruled the ball left Bryan's hand before the seconds ticked down to zero.

"Where's Bryan?" Grady asked sharply, directing the question to Hubie Brown.

"Some reporter wanted to talk to him," Hubie said.

Grady bit back a rebuke. Yelling at Hubie for not telling him sooner wouldn't improve the situation.

"This reporter? Was he a young guy, not too tall, wearing a khaki-colored jacket?"

"Sounds right," Hubie said.

Will Schneider, that same reporter, had interviewed Grady after the game but hadn't mentioned he wanted to talk to Bryan. Damn.

"Hold on," Grady instructed the bus driver. "I'll be right back."

He hurried through the cold night toward the gym, the sound of his own breathing audible.

Bryan should have listened when Grady instructed the players to make a quick exit. He should be on the bus right now, enjoying the victory with his teammates instead of in a hostile environment surrounded by angry fans.

Except Grady knew why Bryan hadn't listened.

The teenager put forth maximum effort in games and practices, but in his other dealings with Grady he gave the minimum. He answered in monosyllables, barely participated in class and didn't try to hide his dislike.

Fans, most of them wearing the orange-and-blue Valley View colors, streamed from the bank of doors. Going against the crowd, Grady finally managed to get inside the school.

With his height, he could see over the heads of most people filling the wide hall outside the gym. He didn't see Bryan but immediately spotted Keri Cassidy standing against a side wall.

He'd picked her out in the stands, too, even though she wore a tan-and-white sweater that should have blended into the surroundings. Every time he turned to talk to his players on the bench during the game, he'd seen her. He hadn't talked to her, though, not even to explain why he hadn't returned her phone call. He headed toward her.

"That was such a great game," Keri practically squealed when she spotted him, her hands in a clapping position. Happiness radiated from her, seeming to be directed at him. As though she was happy *for* him.

"Thanks," he said, wishing he had time to enjoy her enthusiasm. To enjoy her.

"Did you get my message?" she asked.

"I got it, but can we talk about it later? I really need to find Bryan."

"Bryan? I saw him with Will Schneider, the sports reporter from the *Gazette,* a few minutes ago. I didn't want to interrupt so I was waiting to see if I could catch him before he got on the bus."

Somebody waved a notebook as the crowd filed past. Grady caught a glimpse of Schneider's khaki jacket and heard the reporter call, "Congrats again, Coach."

"Interview must be over," Grady said, his uneasiness growing to uncomfortable proportions. "Where were they when you saw them?"

Before she could answer, a teenage boy yelled to

nobody in particular, "Something's going down at the snack bar."

Grady swore under his breath, then headed in the same direction as a half dozen or so teenagers. His height permitted him to see over the gathering crowd to three boys surrounding Bryan. None were as tall as Bryan, but all three outweighed him by at least twenty or thirty pounds.

"You think you're so tough on the court," the largest boy growled. "Let's see how tough you are off it."

Bryan raised the hand that wasn't holding a foil-wrapped hot dog. "Not looking for trouble. Just trying to get something to eat."

Grady started shouldering his way through the crowd but didn't get there fast enough.

The largest boy knocked the hot dog from Bryan's hand. Another shoved him hard enough that he lost his balance and hit the floor. The third boy crowded him, his fist cocked, waiting for Bryan to get up.

"Break it up," Grady yelled.

The boy with the closed fist took a single look at Grady and bellowed, "Run."

He and his buddies scattered like Grady's players when they were afraid he'd throw in another line drill after practice ended. Keri rushed forward, crouching down beside Bryan, worry written on her face as though marked in pen. "Are you okay?"

Bryan gave her a smile that didn't reach his eyes. "Nothing hurt but my pride."

Grady stuck out a hand to help Bryan up. Bryan hesitated, then took the help, probably because Keri was looking on.

"What part of 'get on the bus' didn't you understand?" Grady asked in a low voice when the boy was on his feet.

"It wasn't his fault, Grady," Keri said. "Will Schneider was interviewing him."

Schneider hadn't asked Bryan to treat himself to a hot dog.

"What's going on here?" A physically unimposing security guard wearing glasses and a goatee appeared. He'd been standing near one of the gym entrances during the game, cheering for the home team.

"It's already gone on," Grady said. "The kids causing the trouble have left."

The security guard pointed at Bryan. "Your boy here didn't start it?"

"No, sir," Grady said.

"Then what's he still doing here? The rest of your team got on the bus ten minutes ago."

"Giving an interview," Grady answered, silently conveying to Bryan the boy should let him handle this. "We don't want any more trouble so I'd appreciate you walking with us to the bus."

Grady took Keri's elbow, making sure both Keri and the security guard knew she was included in the request.

The security guard didn't answer but walked toward the exit muttering, "Doesn't have the sense God gave a tick if he's hanging around here after the game he had."

Grady said nothing as he walked with Keri and Bryan behind the security guard. Grady didn't harbor the illusion the security guard would be much help if a fight broke out, but the presence of a man in uniform sometimes deterred trouble.

The security guard didn't stick around once Bryan was safely on the bus, perhaps expecting both Grady and Keri to follow him. Perhaps not.

"I'm walking you to your car," Grady said before Keri could insist she didn't need a chaperone. He held up a finger to the bus driver to indicate he'd be right back. Spotting her Volvo a few aisles away, he walked with her through the parking lot.

"I would have been fine on my own, you know," she said.

"I knew you were going to say that, but think about this. Bryan probably thought he'd be fine, too."

"Thanks for sticking up for him with that security guard," Keri said. "I know you're angry at him so it couldn't have been easy."

"Of course I stuck up for him. He's on my team," he said, then changed the subject. He refused to spend his short time with Keri talking about Bryan. "So why did you call me?"

"Oh!" She turned to face him, and her smile lit up the night. "Rose already has her new prosthesis! She can start using it anytime."

He mentally reviewed his weekend schedule and found it empty aside from the usual preparations for the week's games. "How about tomorrow? Five o'clock at the high school gym?"

"Tomorrow?" She sounded taken aback.

"Sure. The gym clears out late Saturday afternoons. It'll give Rose a chance to try the prosthesis with nobody around before we move to the track at the health club."

"I guess that would be okay," Keri said slowly, pressing

the button on her remote. The Volvo's taillights flashed and the lock to the front door disengaged.

"Great. See you then." He opened the car door and waited for her to climb inside before shutting it again, afraid she might change her mind if he lingered.

The glare Bryan shot him when he got back on the bus couldn't stop Grady from looking forward to Saturday. Working with Rose would be fun and a challenge, but he didn't expect it to be nearly as difficult as the challenge he'd face not letting Keri distract him.

LATE SATURDAY AFTERNOON Keri ventured inside the Springhill High gym with Rose, noting it was as empty as Grady said it would be. Nobody was around. No basketball players. No janitors. Not even Grady.

"I've changed my mind." Rose grabbed her midsection as if she were battling a stomach ache. Her complexion, which should still have been rosy from the cold, was pale. "I don't want to do this."

Rose had uttered those last six words enough times in the past three years it came as no shock to Keri that the girl was balking. The surprise was that she'd agreed in the first place.

"I thought you were on board with this," Keri said. "What changed?"

"I just don't want to." Rose seldom rose her voice and didn't now. "Can we leave?"

"Coach Quinlan's meeting us here."

"Maybe he forgot," she said hopefully at the same time as Grady walked into the gym. He wore Timberlands, jeans and the same brown leather jacket he'd had on the other night, looking as comfortable in the rugged clothing as he did in basketball shorts and a T-shirt. How was it, Keri wondered, that he seemed to grow more attractive each time she saw him?

Grady smiled, held up a finger and called, "Give me a minute."

The janitorial staff had collapsed the bleachers into the back wall, leaving only the bottom row useable. Grady shrugged out of his jacket, sat down and changed into a pair of high-top black basketball shoes before jogging over to join them.

"Hey, Keri." Grady's warm glance chased away the last of the chill Keri had felt from the January air outside the gym. He transferred his attention to Rose, whose hands still cradled her stomach. "Hey, Rose. Where's the prosthesis?"

After a few beats of silence that seemed even more stark in the empty gym, Rose said, "I'm wearing it."

"Great," Grady said enthusiastically. "If you're already walking on it, we'll have you running in no time. So how about talking off those sweats so we can get started?"

The only parts of Rose that moved were her eyes, which darted to Keri. Keri steeled herself against the plea she read in her daughter's gaze. If Rose had decided against learning to use the prosthesis, she'd have to tell Grady herself.

"Something wrong, Rose?" Grady asked.

Rose swallowed, as though the lump in her throat had prevented her from talking. "Do I have to take off my sweats?"

How could Grady teach Rose to effectively use the

prosthesis if she kept the artificial leg covered? His job would be twice as hard. Keri waited for Grady to tell Rose that.

"Not if you don't want to," Grady answered.

Rose's eyes grew wide and...hopeful? "Really?"

"Really," Grady replied. "But you'll want to lose the jacket. It can get hot in here when you're working out."

Rose couldn't get out of the jacket fast enough. Keri took it from her wordlessly, not that she needed to say anything when Grady had the situation under control.

It seemed as though Grady had a sixth sense about Rose, perhaps even guessing the girl never wore shorts, not even in the summer months when the temperature soared into the high eighties and low nineties.

"Let's get started," Grady said. Just like that. No questions about how Rose lost her leg. No sympathy about how difficult it must be to deal with the handicap. No platitudes about how sorry he was. "We'll break it down into steps. The first sounds easier than it is—trust the prosthesis."

"I don't know what you mean," Rose said.

"Imagine my left leg is a prosthesis." Grady got into a runner's crouch, pushed off the hardwood of the gym floor with his right foot and took an exaggerated stride with his left. "Trust that your prosthetic limb will be there when it strikes the ground."

"It won't give out?"

"Absolutely not," Grady said. "Now, you try it."

Keri wandered over to the place where Grady had changed his shoes, took off her own coat and sat down. She habitually carried a book with her. The current one was an exceptionally good romantic suspense that had kept her up late reading the night before. She didn't crack the cover.

She couldn't always hear Grady, but sometimes he'd bend toward Rose and offer encouragement in a gentle voice completely unlike the one he used at basketball practice. Rose would smile up at him, the juxtaposition of the tall, dark man and the young, slender girl touching something inside Keri.

That something turned even more tender at the end of the hour, when Grady jogged very slowly beside Rose as she attempted to run from baseline to baseline. Her movements were jerky, her body and prosthesis not always in sync, but Grady encouraged her every erratic step.

"That was terrific," Grady said when Rose crossed the painted line at the end of the court. "A good note to end on."

Rose was slightly out of breath, perspiration dampening her brow. "But I'm not good at it yet."

"You will be," he said. "Practice—"

Rose groaned, abruptly cutting him off. "Don't say practice makes perfect. That's what Keri says. All the time."

"Keri's right." Grady cast a glance at her and winked broadly. "If something's worth having, it's worth working for."

Was he flirting with her? Keri wondered. Or was she reading too much into an innocent comment? She gathered up her coat and Rose's jacket and walked across the gym to join them.

"Do you grown-ups pass a list of sayings around to use on us kids?" Rose asked Grady in a long-suffering voice.

"Yeah," Grady said. "We call it the LOSS."

"List of Stupid Sayings?" Rose guessed.

"The List of Sassy Sayings," Grady countered in a mock-offended voice.

"Sassy? Now, that's stupid." Rose giggled, a high-pitched sound that seemed to fill the gym.

"Here's another saying—after we work out, there'll be food," Grady said. "What do you say, Rose? How 'bout I take you and Keri to Bernie's Grill? I'll buy."

"I love Bernie's," Rose said.

Keri loved the idea of going to dinner with Grady, but his idea wasn't doable. "You're supposed to be at Taylor Garrity's house in fifteen minutes, Rose. We have just enough time for you to go home and change clothes."

Rose let loose another groan, this one louder than before. "I forgot." To Grady, she said, "We need to finish up a group science project that's due Monday."

"It's a study party," Keri said. At least, she hoped that's what it would turn out to be. Rose's grades were good. Her social life wasn't. "They're sending out for pizza, too."

"We'll do it another time, then," Grady said, then casually directed his next question at Keri. "What about you? Got plans for dinner?"

Bryan was going out with friends this evening, so Keri planned to fix a salad or something easy for dinner and eat in front of the television. Earlier she'd picked up a Hugh Grant movie at the video store.

"Nothing I can't change," she said. "But I'm the one who should be buying."

His hazel eyes twinkled mischievously, giving her a glimpse of the boy he must have been. "Are you saying you'll go with me if I let you pay?"

She smiled at him. She couldn't help herself. "I guess I am."

"Deal," he said so quickly that she laughed, sounding nearly as young and carefree as Rose had.

CHAPTER SEVEN

BERNIE'S GRILL WAS PACKED. Families with small children sat at tables adjacent to groups of teenagers, many of whom were on Grady's basketball team. Not the best place to take a woman you wanted to get to know better.

"We can go somewhere else," Grady told Keri.

She'd met him at the restaurant at a prearranged time. She'd changed clothes, too, into winter-white jeans and a pale pink pullover sweater that brought out the warm tones in her skin. Now she stood beside him waiting for a waitress to clear off a table somewhere in the back of the restaurant.

"Why go somewhere else?" Keri asked.

"It's kind of crowded here," he pointed out.

"Springhill isn't very big," she said. "On Saturday night at dinnertime, every place is crowded."

He made a mental note to take her someplace outside of Springhill the next time they had dinner together. The trick was getting her to agree to a second time.

The restaurant was oddly shaped, with occasional nooks shooting off from the main dining area. A middle-aged waitress signaled them to follow her to a table for two crammed into one of the alcoves, which would give them a modicum of privacy. Grady felt the eyes of almost everyone in the place on them. Some patrons smiled at him, possibly because his basketball team was on a six-game winning streak. A couple of boys near the door pointed.

"Do you remember me?" the waitress asked Keri after they were seated and she took their drink orders. She had a square build and an open, florid face. "Carol Frost. We worked the concession stand together last year. My daughter Megan was a Springhill cheerleader."

Recognition flashed across Keri's face. "Oh, yes. Megan was a senior last year, right? Where is she now?"

"At Pitt, doing really well, but she misses cheering," Carol said. "I haven't been to many games this year, but I hear your boy's lighting it up. He was just in here with some buddies."

"No girls?" Keri asked.

"There were girls," Carol said with a hearty laugh. "There are always girls when Bryan's here, and he's here a lot."

That spoke well for the restaurant, Grady thought. "He must like your burgers."

"He likes getting them on the house," Carol said in a stage whisper. "Bernie told us not to take his money."

Grady couldn't keep quiet, not when the restaurant's practice of treating one of his players differently from everybody else went against every value he was trying to impart. "Then Bernie should change his policy."

"What Bernie does is Bernie's business," Carol said, her smile dimming. Keri's smile had completely disappeared. "I'll be back in a little while to take your orders."

The instant Carol was out of earshot, Keri asked him in a tight voice, "Did you have to say that?"

"Yeah, I did." He rubbed the side of his jaw while he considered the best way to make her understand. "Bryan's already getting interest letters from college coaches, right?"

She frowned, obviously puzzled at the direction he was taking the conversation. "He has a pretty thick stack of them."

"That's why I said what I said." He looked directly into her eyes to make sure she realized the significance of what he was about to tell her. "I don't want him to get in trouble once the recruiting heats up. It's against NCAA rules for college recruiters to offer freebies. Bryan needs to get in the habit now of not accepting something for nothing."

It couldn't lead to anything good. Grady had firsthand knowledge of that.

Keri's tight-lipped expression didn't change. "So you think Bernie gives Bryan free food because he's good at basketball?"

Yeah, he did. "Got another explanation?"

"How about this? Bernie was dating Maddy before she died. I imagine treating Maddy's kids to burgers is his way of honoring her memory."

If their table hadn't been so small, Grady might have crawled under it. He grimaced. "I'm sorry. I didn't know."

Her shoulders relaxed, and her expression lost its fierceness. "How could you? I keep forgetting you haven't been coaching the team long. I shouldn't expect you to automatically know what kind of kid Bryan is."

The kind used to being treated like a god because he could toss a basketball through a hoop, Grady thought. That wasn't entirely accurate in this case, but he'd witnessed plenty of examples of favoritism since he'd taken over the head coaching job at Springhill High.

"Speaking of Bryan," she said casually. Too casually. "He said you're mulling over what to do about the incident at the concession stand."

"That's right." He wasn't in a hurry to decide on the repercussions of Bryan disregarding his order, preferring to let Bryan stew over what those consequences might be.

"Why do you have to do anything?" she asked.

Wasn't the answer obvious? "Because he didn't do what I told him to do."

"But he already learned his lesson." She sounded like a lawyer in court presenting closing arguments to the jurors. "You saw how white his face got when those boys surrounded him. They really gave him a scare."

"On my team, actions have consequences."

The return of the waitress bearing soft drinks interrupted their conversation. They placed their orders, a quarter-pound hamburger for her, a half-pound cheeseburger for him with an order of fries to share.

"Just go easy on him, okay?" Keri said when they were alone again. "Don't suspend him or anything."

Grady had already decided Bryan's actions didn't warrant a suspension so the promise was easy to make. "I won't suspend him."

Her chest contracted, as though she'd been holding her breath while waiting for his answer. "That's good."

"Then can we talk about something else?" he asked.

"What do you want to talk about?" She put her elbows on the table. Her green eyes contained little flecks of gold, and her smattering of freckles was so light he had to look close to see them. He liked looking closely at her.

"You. I've known you for three weeks, and you're still a mystery."

She smiled, revealing the appealing space between her straight white teeth. "Me? A mystery? Let's see if I can clear that up for you. I grew up in Richmond, Virginia, with terrific parents and a brother I don't see often enough. I majored in advertising at VCU. I work at the *Springhill Gazette*. And I've got two kids I'm crazy about. End of story."

"That's barely the beginning," he said. "You didn't even tell me how you ended up in Springhill."

She grew silent, swirling the plastic straw in her cola before she answered, "Did you know Tony and I used to be engaged?"

"I heard that," he said, but didn't tell her Mary Lynn had been the one to tell him.

"I met him in Fort Lauderdale, right before I graduated from college. We were staying at the same hotel and I thought he was cute." She rolled her eyes, although Grady wasn't sure why. "We dated long-distance for a while, then he asked me to marry him. I thought we should live in the same city first so I applied for a job at the *Gazette* and I got it. I wanted to get to know his friends, his family." She paused. "Come to think of it, it's strange I never met you."

"Not so strange," Grady said. "Tony and I grew up in different parts of Pennsylvania. I only knew what was happening with him when my mom told me. I'm not sure she ever mentioned you."

"We were only together about a year," Keri said.

"Mind me asking why you broke up?"

Her smile looked sad. "I thought you didn't want to talk about Bryan."

"What does Bryan have to do with it?"

"Not just Bryan. Rose, too," she said. "Let's just say our relationship wasn't strong enough to survive the shock of me suddenly having two half-grown kids."

Carol Frost arrived with burgers and fries. The waitress exchanged more pleasantries with Keri, but Grady was silent, imagining what a difficult time that must have been for Keri. He knew she was twenty-five and had taken custody of Bryan and Rose three years ago. So she'd become a single mother with two children less than a year after graduating from college and landing her first job.

The fragrant smell of the food teased his nostrils, but he couldn't eat until he had a better understanding of what she'd been through. "How did you know Bryan and Rose's mom?"

"We worked together. Maddy was this larger-than-life character, always up for getting together with friends, always making room at the dinner table for one more. A lot of times that was me." She adopted a wistful expression. "She was like the big sister I never had. Rose and Bryan even started calling me Aunt Keri."

"What happened?" he asked softly, trusting she'd know he was asking about the car accident.

She kneaded the space between her eyes before answering. "Maddy picked up Rose from school to take her to the dentist. It had rained that morning but the temperature was dropping, and the crews hadn't salted all the roads. She hit a patch of ice and slid off the road, straight into a tree. The cops said she wasn't even speeding."

Recognizing that the loss of her friend still pained her,

he reached across the table and squeezed her hand. If Keri needed support now, he thought, she must have been desperate for it back then.

"How could Tony not have stood by you?" He didn't catch on that he'd asked the question aloud until she answered.

"He did. For a little while," she said. "To be fair, we'd never talked about whether we wanted kids of our own. Then suddenly I was responsible for somebody else's."

"Why did you seek custody?"

"Bryan and Rose didn't have anyone else. Tony suggested foster care, but I couldn't do that. Maddy was a foster child, and she hated being shuffled from home to home. I couldn't let that happen to her children."

She told the story matter-of-factly, as though she didn't realize what a remarkable thing she'd done for her friend's children.

"What about their father?" he asked.

She lowered her voice to a whisper. "He died a long time ago. Shot trying to rob a convenience store."

"Jesus," Grady said, horror coursing through him. "Do the kids know?"

"Yeah, but they don't talk about him. He was never a part of their lives so I'm not sure they even think about him. At least, I hope they don't." She picked up a French fry, put it down. "So now you know my story. Mystery solved."

They ate companionably for the better part of the next hour while he tried to find out more about Keri. He learned her parents had been happily married for thirty years and that her father had cosigned the loan for the house she bought after she adopted Bryan and Rose.

She told him about her brother's recent engagement. Her whirlwind trip to Virginia over the Christmas holidays, where her family showered her and the kids with gifts. Her determination to save money for a college fund.

"Enough about me," she said after they were through eating. "Tell me how you ended up driving a truck."

"It's a boring story," he said evasively, the bitter taste of his experience at Carolina State more pungent than the cheeseburger. He'd tell her about his past once she knew him better. But not yet.

"Try me," she pressed.

Because he clearly had to say something, he opted for a version of the truth. "I needed to clear my head, and the open road seemed like a good place to do it."

"But why did you—"

The cell phone in her purse played the beginning notes of a song he'd heard on the radio that was popular with teenagers. But then, Keri was only six years removed from being a teenager herself.

"Sorry, but I've got to see who's calling," she told Grady as she was fishing the phone out of her purse. She checked the display, the faint lines reappearing on her forehead. "It's Rose."

"Hello," Keri said. The phone at her ear, she listened intently for a moment. "Now?"

She closed her eyes briefly at Rose's reply.

"Sure. Be there in five." Keri broke the connection. "I'm sorry, but I've got to pick up Rose."

"Everything okay?"

"I think so." She dropped the cell phone back into her

purse, her movements quick and efficient. "But she really wants to go home."

"You wish she'd stay," he observed.

"I wish she'd try to make friends. You saw her today. She's fun, funny. I don't think she lets other kids see that side of her."

She stood up and removed her coat from the back of the chair where she'd draped it. Then she dug her wallet from her purse.

"You go ahead. I'll take care of the check," Grady said.

"No." She took out some money and put it in front of him on the table. "I've got to have some way to thank you for working with Rose."

"How do you know it's not a ploy to get you to go out with me?" he asked.

"Because I saw you with her." She leaned very close to him and whispered, "And who said you needed a ploy, anyway?"

He felt her breath against his mouth, smelled her light, feminine scent and felt the connection between them as strongly as if they'd been bound by a rope. He smiled at her long and slow. "Does this mean you'll go out with me next Saturday?"

"Yes." She came so close to him that he could almost feel her lips touching his. "It does."

THE SCENT OF FRESHLY BAKED bread filled the sub shop, but Bryan had never seen it emptier.

There were no clusters of high school girls gossiping at the tables, no loudmouthed boys yucking it up and no clerk behind the counter.

Most notably, there was no Jackie Fitzgibbons.

In Spanish class he'd overheard Jackie making plans to meet some other students after school. When classes let out for the day, it seemed like a good idea to head on over to the fast-food restaurant, stroll in and act surprised to run into her.

Bryan hadn't counted on being surprised *not* to see her. Dan Domenici, his mop of dark hair tied back in a short ponytail, emerged from the back of the shop carrying a tray of pickle slices. As a senior on the basketball team the year before, he'd gotten the nickname Double D. Now everybody called Dan's younger brother, Andy, who was on the team this year, Single D.

"Hey, B-ry." Only Double D ever called Bryan that. "What you doin' here?"

Fat white snowflakes drifted to the ground, visible through the glass windows in the front of the shop. The forecast called for a couple of inches of snow by nightfall.

"The snow keeping business away?" Bryan asked.

"Not what I meant," Double D said. "Why aren't you at practice?"

Bryan shrugged. "I'll get there."

"You better get there quick. I hear that new coach doesn't take nothin' from nobody."

Bryan made a noncommittal sound. He didn't feel like talking about Coach Quinlan, not after everybody and his brother had told him the coach had been with Keri Saturday night.

"I hear Keri went out with him this weekend," Double D said.

"She was thanking him for doing something nice for my sister," Bryan mumbled, repeating what Keri had told him.

"That's not the way I heard it. I heard they were practically drooling over each other."

Bryan butted up against the counter, ready to leap over it. "Don't talk about Keri like that."

Double D backed up. "Sorry, man. I didn't mean nothin' by it."

The fight went out of Bryan. "It's not true, anyway," he said, hoping he was right.

"Okay. Okay."

Bryan ordered a six-inch sub even though he wasn't hungry and stuck around for a while talking ball with Double D to prove Coach didn't scare him. Yeah, the coach had suspended him before. But that was for a game against a nondistrict opponent, when the outcome didn't count in the standings.

Johnson Heights, tomorrow night's opponent, was in Springhill's district. While not a powerhouse, Johnson Heights wasn't a walkover, either. Coach Hard-Ass would be steamed at Bryan for getting to practice late, but he wouldn't make a big deal out of a measly thirty minutes.

As it turned out, it was more like thirty-five. Bryan's teammates were running a closeout shooting drill, where one guy rushed the player taking the shot to get him used to defensive pressure. Bryan joined the line, acting as though he'd been at practice all along.

A few teammates slanted him wary looks, probably afraid Coach would make the entire team run because Bryan was late. But the rest of the practice proceeded just like every other. Running, more shooting, working on defense, putting in a new play on offense, more running.

"First player to hit two free throws ends the practice,"

Coach Quinlan said. "Hit one of two or oh of two and we all run."

Bryan was the third player at the line and the first to knock down two consecutive shots.

"That's it," Coach said. "Be at the gym tomorrow at six."

Bryan didn't push his luck. He headed toward the locker room, a bounce to his step even though it had been a hard practice.

"Charleton!" Coach Quinlan bellowed before he was in the clear. "Get over here!"

The coach's voice reverberated inside Bryan, churning up the sub he shouldn't have eaten. Be cool, he told himself. Bryan raised his chin and ambled over to the coach.

"You owe me a suicide for every five minutes you were late. Get on the line and start running."

Thirty-five minutes late, Bryan thought. Seven suicides. He was in great shape. He could handle that. His lungs felt like they were burning by the last two, but he didn't slow down. Damn if he'd let the coach know he was having difficulty. As soon as he finished the final one, he filed past the coach, not bothering to look at him.

"We're not through, Charleton."

Bryan stopped, turned around.

"That's two times in four days you've caused me trouble. You're not getting off with a little running. I'm benching you for the first quarter tomorrow."

The anger Bryan had been keeping in check burst free. "You can't do that!"

"Make that the first half. Say another word, and you'll sit out the game."

Bryan bit down on his anger, directed a mutinous glare at the coach, then stalked to the locker room.

First Jackie hadn't been at the sub shop and now this, which was so much worse. The hell of it was that he almost had Jackie convinced to come to the game tomorrow. He'd wanted to impress her, but he couldn't do that from the bench.

"Great," Bryan muttered sarcastically under his breath. "Just great."

Another problem was what to tell Keri. He didn't want her finding out he'd been deliberately late to practice, especially after the incident at the concession stand.

Better to leave her a note that coach was benching him for the first half and let her draw her own conclusions.

KERI STOPPED IN FRONT of the woman selling tickets at the door of Tuesday night's basketball game and flashed her athletic booster pass. For a flat donation, the pass got her into every Springhill High home sporting event.

"First quarter's already over," the woman said, then cocked her head. "You're Bryan Charleton's mom, aren't you?"

"Yes," Keri said politely, trying to figure out how she knew the woman and coming up blank.

"Betsy Graber," she said, as though that was any help at all. "You might want to tell Coach Quinlan to play your boy more."

"What makes you think he'd listen?"

"You were with him Saturday night, weren't you?" Betsy asked the very question Keri had been trying all day to avoid. She'd heard it at work, from a neighbor and now here at the gym she instantly saw was packed. Good.

She'd deliberately arrived late to avoid sitting with her usual crowd. And Rose, once again, had declined to come with her.

"Have a nice evening," she told Betsy Graber. She was tempted to crawl under the bleachers and watch the rest of the game from a crouch but headed for the bank of seats nearest the door, away from the jam-packed section where the home crowd sat.

She waited for a break in the action, then followed a trim, athletic-looking young man up the bleacher stairs. She'd noticed him getting out of his car while she was searching for a parking spot. He sat down in the top row in one of the few seats left in the gym. She sat next to him, exchanging an impersonal smile.

Sensing an upset in the making, most of the people around them shouted and applauded in approval after a Johnson Heights player hit a jump shot to knot the score. Keri remained silent.

"I take it you're rooting for Springhill?" the man beside her asked. He had regular features, a friendly smile and a nice way about him.

"Go, Cougars," she said.

He grinned. "Maybe you can tell me why Bryan Charleton's still in his warm-ups."

Because Grady didn't know what going easy on a player meant. Bryan had only let her know he was being benched for the first half this morning, probably anticipating that she'd be angry. She was angry, all right. But not with Bryan.

"Coach Quinlan's the only one who can answer that," she said with a forced smile.

Interest bloomed on his face. "Coach Robert Quinlan?"

She shook her head. "Grady Quinlan."

The man craned his neck to see around some fans below them who had leapt to their feet after another Johnson Heights basket. Grady paced the sidelines in navy slacks and a blue dress shirt, his tie loosened at the neck, his sport jacket discarded. "Are you sure? I've only seen newspaper photos of Robert Quinlan, but that sure looks like him."

"I'm sure," Keri said.

"So he didn't coach at Carolina State?"

It occurred to Keri that Grady never had answered her question about which college he'd played for. But if he'd coached, too, surely he would have mentioned that. "Not that I know of."

The man shrugged. "Must be a different Quinlan."

He took out a clipboard, leaned back against the wall and started taking notes. She read the Penn State insignia on his white polo shirt and realized he was a college recruiter.

She wasn't entirely up to speed on NCAA rules but knew recruiters were only permitted direct contact with high school players and their families during what were known as live periods. High school basketball season was a dead time.

To avoid getting the personable young man in trouble, she said nothing for the rest of the closely fought half.

After the players left the court, the Penn State scout stood. "I'm about to brave the line at the concession stand. I'll get you anything you want if you save my seat."

"You'll want to find another seat after I tell you who I am."

The man's gaze roamed over her face. "Come on. There isn't a seat in the house with a better view."

She couldn't help but feel flattered. "I'm Bryan Charleton's mom."

"Whoa. Aren't you kind of young?"

She had to smile at the shock on his face. "His *adoptive* mom."

"Well, I've gotta tell you. That's the first time I'm okay with one of my lame lines not working."

She laughed at his comment.

Once the second half started, Bryan played as if he had something to prove, hitting his first three shots to put Springhill ahead. The Cougars never trailed again, giving Keri plenty of time to think about Grady's evasiveness. He hadn't satisfactorily explained why he'd taken a job driving a truck and never had told her what he'd been doing beforehand.

Questions swirled through her mind. Could Grady be related to Robert Quinlan? What had Robert Quinlan done to land himself in the newspaper?

With a few minutes remaining in the game, Springhill had a lead commanding enough that Keri slipped out early. She checked on Rose once she was home, then switched on her computer, signed on to the Internet and navigated to her favorite search engine.

She typed "Robert Quinlan" and "Carolina State" in the search engine. The first item that popped up was a newspaper story from the *Raleigh News and Observer* that was dated more than a year ago.

Quinlan fired after recruiting scandal read the headline.

She scanned the story. Robert Quinlan, an assistant basketball coach at Carolina State, had reportedly given student athletes and prospects impermissible benefits from a special fund made fat by booster donations. The benefits included cash, free travel, meals, housing and basketball tickets.

The NCAA Committee on Infractions placed Carolina State on probation but didn't issue more penalties because the head coach proclaimed his innocence, insisting Quinlan had acted alone.

Keri hit the back button on her server, looking more closely at the screen of results. On more than one occasion, Robert Quinlan was referred to as Robert G. Quinlan.

Her heart beating hard, she maneuvered her mouse so the arrow on the screen pointed to the search engine's images tool. Her finger hovered above the mouse, shaking slightly, before she clicked.

A dozen photos of a brown-haired, hazel-eyed handsome man appeared on her oversize flat screen. She blinked, but the images didn't change.

Robert G. Quinlan wasn't a man who had the same last name as Grady.

He *was* Grady.

CHAPTER EIGHT

THE SECURITY GUARD AT THE *Springhill Gazette* tapped his fingertips to a staccato beat on the smooth surface of the downstairs desk as Grady approached. He was a beefy, strongly built man in his thirties whose name tag said his name was Chester.

"I know who you are," Chester said before Grady could identify himself. "Coach Quinlan."

"That's right." It no longer surprised Grady when strangers recognized him. Any coach of a team as successful as the Springhill Cougars, whose record now stood at 18-1, could tell you it came with the territory.

"I played for Springhill fifteen years ago," Chester said, a faraway look briefly touching his eyes. "Still catch most of the games. Want some advice?"

"I've got a feeling you're going to give it even if I don't."

Chester let loose with a good-natured belly laugh. "You're right. But you're wrong keeping Charleton on the bench. You won last night, but you won't keep winning if you don't play that boy heavy minutes."

"Some things are more important than winning," Grady said, which earned him a look of disbelief from Chester. "You know if Keri Cassidy is still here?"

"She's working late tonight," Chester said, still regarding him skeptically. "Third floor. Take the elevator. I'll let her know you're on your way up."

"Thanks," Grady said.

En route to the elevator he flipped open his cell phone to listen one more time to Keri's message. Just to make sure he'd heard it right.

"Grady, it's Keri. Rose won't be coming to the health club tonight. I appreciate your help, but I've decided to find a physical therapist to work with her."

That was the entire message. The original plan had been for Bryan to drop his sister off at the Springhill Health Club after basketball practice for her second workout session. Keri was supposed to join Grady and Rose when she finished up at work.

The elevator doors slid open. Grady entered the car, flipping his phone closed. What had caused Keri to change her mind? And why hadn't she specified a reason? It didn't make sense.

After a short ride, the elevator doors opened. Grady stepped onto a floor that seemed deserted. Desk chairs sat empty in front of dark computer screens in work areas set apart by cubicles. Grady hadn't bothered to change from his basketball shoes after practice and heard his soft footfalls on the tiled floor.

He caught the gleam of a computer monitor out of the corner of his eye, then heard the ringing of a telephone. Chester had been slow in announcing his arrival, he guessed.

Keri picked up the receiver, then turned to watch him approach, no smile of welcome on her face. She hung up the phone. "What are you doing here?"

Yes, something was definitely wrong.

"I came to talk to you about the message you left on my cell," he said. "I thought I might catch you before you left work."

"Give me a minute." She turned back to her computer screen, and he looked over her shoulder. She was working on an ad for the oddly named Froggers Gardening Center and Nursery, but she'd made the name work to advantage. A cartoonish green frog stuck out one of its front legs, from which protruded a comically oversize thumb. The caption read: *We'll help you get your own.*

"That's good," Grady said with a smile. "Don't let me keep you from finishing. I can wait."

"I'm already done." She switched off the computer and swiveled in her chair, her face a blank mask. "There's nothing for us to talk about. I'm finding someone else to work with Rose."

To give himself time to figure out what might be behind her change of heart, Grady lowered himself so he sat on the edge of her desk. Nothing occurred to him.

"I won't be able to make our date Saturday night, either," she said, another baffling blow.

"How 'bout a rain check?" he asked.

"That wouldn't be a good idea."

Grady had been rejected before, but never so coldly. Hiding his disappointment, he asked the pertinent question. "Why not?"

She lifted her head, met his eyes. "I know about Carolina State. I know what you did, and I know why you were fired."

If somebody had hurled a boulder at him, it wouldn't

have hurt worse than her words. An advantage of living in Springhill was nobody held his past against him. Although Grady had always known his link to Carolina State would surface, he hadn't anticipated Keri casting the first stone once it did.

"Don't you have anything to say?" she asked.

Grady had said plenty when NCAA investigators descended on Carolina State with charges of recruiting violations. Especially after Bud Hardgrove, the college's charismatic, well-liked head coach, sent them knocking at Grady's door. Hardgrove claimed Grady enticed top high school prospects to play basketball at Carolina State with money from a slush fund.

Grady assumed then that defending himself would make a difference. He told the investigators the fund was so secret he had no idea it existed. He theorized that Hardgrove had offered him up as the fall guy to cover his own transgressions.

After he got fired, he quickly discovered the only people who believed him were the ones who already believed *in* him. How stupid he'd been to start counting Keri among that group.

"Why should I say anything?" he asked, hearing the edge to his voice. "Seems to me you've already made up your mind."

"I read the newspaper stories, Grady." Her voice was flinty, inviting no argument.

It struck him that Keri worked for a newspaper so he shouldn't be surprised she was siding with her editorial counterparts. The rationalization didn't help.

"How'd you find out?" If word of the scandal was spreading through Springhill, he had to prepare himself.

"From a Penn State recruiter at last night's game."

He digested the information, not only weighing how it affected him but how it pertained to Keri. "It's against the rules for those guys to talk to you or Bryan until the high school season's over."

"And you're such a stickler for the rules," she countered. "Tell me something. How do you justify coming down so hard on Bryan after what you did?"

"I don't think I am coming down hard on him."

"You suspend him for something he didn't do, then bench him for buying a hot dog."

Grady hadn't expected Bryan to share the entire story of why he'd gotten benched, but still he felt disappointed in the boy. "Bryan must not have told you everything," he began.

"Oh, yeah." She smacked her forehead. "Bryan didn't listen when you ordered him on the bus. Never mind that he was talking to a reporter. What happens if Bryan does something really terrible, like forgetting his shooting shirt? Will you kick him off the team?"

He didn't interrupt her diatribe, annoyed at himself for attempting to explain. Spots of color stained her cheeks and her chest heaved. Keri had made up her mind about him, and nothing he could say would change it.

"Are you through?" he asked.

After a short pause, she nodded.

"Then it's my turn. Believe what you want about me, but don't punish Rose."

"I'm not—".

He held up a hand. "You told me you sock away every penny you can for college. You don't have the money for a physical therapist. It'd stretch your budget so thin you'd have to cut down on other things. Either way, Rose loses."

She was quiet for a moment, digesting that. Finally, she asked, "What are you proposing?"

"Let me keep working with her. You saw her the other night. She made amazing progress. Don't take that away from her."

Silence reigned, so absolute he could hear the hum of the lights overhead. Then she said, "Okay."

He nodded once. "I'll see myself out."

He waited until the elevator doors closed to shut his eyes and lean his head against the padded wall at the back of the car.

He supposed he should take consolation in his minor victory, but all he felt was a crushing sense of loss.

ROSE ORDERED A DOUBLE scoop of strawberry-and-vanilla frozen custard from the friendly woman behind the counter, then resumed the stream of chatter that had started when Keri picked her up at the health club.

"Coach Q said I was doing amazing," she said, using her nickname for Grady. "He said he's going to start calling me Zoom Zoom, like that car in the commercial." She giggled. "Coach Q thinks I can be really fast."

Keri hadn't talked to Grady in the week since he'd confronted her at the newspaper office, but she heard about him constantly. Especially on the days he worked with Rose and her new prosthesis.

"Coach Q said it was too cold for frozen custard, but I told him that was because he hadn't been to Muffett's," Rose said, gesturing at the bright little shop where they were the only customers. "We should have asked him to come with us. You like him, don't you?"

Keri had started to like him, quite a lot, actually. But she'd always bought into that line about judging a man by the content of his character.

"I don't know him very well," she said evasively.

"I know Bryan doesn't like him, even though that makes zero sense with the team winning like it is," Rose continued. The Cougars' record was 20-1, with nine of the victories coming after Grady began coaching the team. "Coach Q's really nice."

"So you've said." Over and over again.

Rose tilted her head. "You should come out and watch next time we have a workout."

"We'll see." Keri still had a lot to learn about being a parent, but she'd figured out those two words were magic.

"Here you go." The clerk handed Rose her double cone, then filled Keri's order for a single scoop of chocolate. They completed the transaction just as the bell signaled the arrival of another customer.

Tony Marco, his dark hair and mustache dotted with quickly melting snowflakes, strode into the store.

"Rose. Keri." Tony's step didn't falter as he marched right up to them, as though supremely confident of his welcome. "When it comes to frozen custard, great appetites must think alike."

Rose stopped licking her frozen treat to issue a smile and a greeting. "Hi, Mr. Marco."

Keri nodded a silent hello. She'd done a pretty good job over the past month of avoiding Tony, but Springhill wasn't a big place. She couldn't dodge him forever.

"So how's my girl doing?" Tony asked.

At first Keri thought Tony was addressing her, but he'd directed his question at Rose. In those first few weeks after the accident, Tony had been a steady presence, lending his support to Rose and staying with Bryan while Keri kept overnight vigils in Rose's hospital room. Both teenagers still liked him. Keri hadn't confided in them, nor would she ever, why Tony broke their engagement.

"I'm grr-eat." Rose sounded nearly as animated as the cartoon tiger in the cereal commercials. "I'm going out for the track team."

"That's wonderful," Tony said, but confusion clouded his features.

Rose answered his unasked question. "Did you know I got a sports prosthesis?"

Keri started. Rose never, ever brought up her amputated leg when they were out in public. Not even to people she considered friends.

"Wow." Tony slanted a pointed look at Keri. "Somebody needs to pick up a phone and tell me these things."

The irony of Tony's statement wasn't lost on Keri. If Tony hadn't broken their engagement, he'd know everything there was to know about Bryan and Rose. She could have pointed that out but didn't see what the purpose would be. She'd long ago fallen out of love with Tony Marco.

"Why would I?" Keri asked.

"Because we're friends." He gazed directly into her eyes the way he used to, trying to create intimacy between them when it no longer existed.

Their supposed friendship was news to Keri, but she

couldn't think of a way to disagree with him while Rose was listening. While she was puzzling over how to answer, the bell over the door sounded again.

Keri turned to see Mary Lynn Marco gaping at them as though the February chill had frozen her tongue. A cold wind carrying powdery white snowflakes gusted at her back, rustling her long, curly hair and the plastic shopping bag she carried. It bore the name of the drugstore next door.

Seeming to become aware she still held the door open, she stepped all the way into the shop and let it close behind her. She wore a leopard-print coat with a fake-fur collar, but Keri could still see her lungs fill with air. Throwing her shoulders back, Mary Lynn lifted her chin and ventured forward, her smile as fake as the ones painted on department store mannequins.

"There you are," she said to Tony, putting her hand on his arm, the leather of her gloves tightening. "I thought you were going to wait for me in the car."

"I felt like getting some frozen custard," Tony muttered, obviously not happy to see her.

His statement cast more doubt on their supposed coincidental meeting. Keri figured it was likely Tony had spotted her and Rose entering the shop and followed them.

Nobody said anything for a moment, spurring Keri to act. She extended the hand not holding her frozen custard. "Hi, Mary Lynn. I'm thrilled to finally get a chance to meet you."

Okay, she might have gone overboard. But how do you convey to a wife you're not interested in her husband when her husband won't leave you alone?

"Hi," Mary Lynn said coolly, shaking Keri's hand without enthusiasm and with her gloves still on.

"And this is Rose, my daughter," Keri said.

"Hi, Rose." A smile transformed Mary Lynn's face from merely pretty to beautiful. "You have the most gorgeous hair. I'd do anything to have mine long and straight like yours."

Rose fingered strands of her golden-brown hair with the hand not holding her frozen custard. "Thanks, but I think yours is pretty."

"How sweet of you to say," Mary Lynn said, as though she didn't believe her. She couldn't maintain her smile when she tilted her face up to her husband's. "So what were you all talking about?"

Tony shifted from foot to foot like a guilty man, then said, "Rose's new sports prosthesis."

Keri glanced quickly at Rose, but the girl didn't react to Tony openly discussing her handicap.

"Cool," Mary Lynn said.

"Coach Q says I'll be ready in time to try out for track," Rose supplied.

"Coach Quinlan? Tony's cousin?" Mary Lynn sounded surprised. "What does he have to do with this?"

"He's helping me learn to run," Rose said proudly.

"He's a very good guy," Mary Lynn said instantly. "In fact, it's hard for me to believe some woman hasn't snapped him up." She looked pointedly at Keri. "You're single, aren't you?"

"Yes," Keri said slowly.

"Then you should let Tony and me fix you up," Mary Lynn said pleasantly.

Tony's flush started at the base of his neck and worked

its way up to his eyebrows by the time he took Mary Lynn by the elbow. "Come on, Mary Lynn, we've got to be going."

"But you didn't get your frozen custard," she said.

"I'm not hungry anymore. See you around, Keri, Rose."

"Bye, Mr. Marco, Mrs. Marco," Rose called after them. She took a long lick of her ice cream, which had started to drip. "I think that's a really good idea."

Keri didn't like the gleam in her eye. "What?"

"You should totally date Coach Q. That would be so cool. But you don't need the Marcos to fix you up. I'll do it."

"Stop right there." Keri held up a hand. "I do not need my teenage daughter to get me dates."

Rose's eyebrows lifted. "You sure about that? If I set you up, you'd actually have a date."

Keri put her hands on her hips and feigned indignation. "Gee, thanks, Miss Match dot com."

Rose giggled, which had been Keri's intention. Anything to get the girl off the topic of Grady Quinlan. And Keri's mind off the man.

CHAPTER NINE

THE HEAD COACH OF THE Springhill High basketball team, Grady discovered, was expected to do more than run practices and win games.

One of his social obligations was to show up at the Springhill Bowlarama and Laser Tag on the second Saturday night in February, which happened to be the weekend before the district play-offs.

"You can't *not* go on Springhill basketball night," Tony had told Grady, explaining that a portion of every dollar spent would be donated to the boys' basketball program. "It's tradition. Besides, it'll be fun. You really turned public opinion around with all those wins."

John Sessions, the craggy-faced, middle-aged owner of the facility, seemed to be at the forefront of Grady's new fan base. He pumped Grady's hand in a hearty shake.

"You're doing a hell of a job," he said. "Nothing can stop us from getting that state championship."

Grady tried not to groan, the same battle he fought every time he heard that sentiment. "We have to get through districts and regionals first. Anything can happen on any given night."

Sessions erupted into deep-throated laughter. "Listen to

you. We're 20-1, and we only lost the one because you didn't play Bryan Charleton. You won't be making that mistake in the play-offs."

Sessions slapped him on the back, which wasn't the first time that had happened tonight. Grady's popularity seemed to have increased in direct proportion to his team's win-loss record. News had broken that he and Tony were cousins and it hadn't caused a single ripple. But not everybody loved a winner, Grady thought as he caught sight of Keri Cassidy in the distance.

His eyes had gone unerringly to her even though she was some ways away from him. The hell of it was he still itched to prove to her what kind of a guy he really was.

He stepped past the front desk into the main part of the bowling alley and passed the snack bar, where he smelled French fries and grilled burgers and hot dogs. People of various ages filled every available lane, the sounds of bowling balls crashing into pins a constant cacophony. Teenagers congregated around the banks of video game machines stationed at one end of the lanes, the machines flashing lights and emitting shrill sounds.

"You're here!" Rose disengaged from the pack of teens and rushed up to him, taking him by the hand. "The basketball players are getting ready to pick teams for the laser tag tournament."

Grady laughed at her effusive greeting and let her tug him along. "You're not suggesting I play?"

Rose glanced back over her shoulder, her face comically scrunched. "You *have* to play. The head coach always plays."

"How about sisters? Can they play?"

"Some do," she said.

"Then if I'm playing, so are you."

Her dark eyes turned huge, but he read hope in them instead of fear. "Do you think I'm ready?"

"Sure do. We'll ask them to wait, then I'll run you home for your sports prosthesis."

He had to strain to hear Rose's voice when she replied. "We don't have to. I wore it."

"Way to go, Rose." He enjoyed the way her face flushed at his praise. "So, what are you waiting for? Let's kick some laser tag butt."

The laser tag arena had clearly been built as an addition to the bowling alley, if only because it stretched to two stories. A crowd of mostly teenagers gathered near the briefing room, including what appeared to be the entire Springhill basketball team. The only adults present were Tony and Mary Lynn Marco, the junior varsity basketball coach and Keri.

Grady caught Keri's eye and nodded. She nodded back. Attraction slammed into him. With her brown hair tumbling to her shoulders and her sweater clinging to her slim shape, she looked delectable. And completely inaccessible.

Rose let go of his hand, rushed up to Keri and whispered something in her ear. From the way Keri smiled, Grady guessed Rose had told her she was going to play.

"We'll have four teams of six players each." Tony Marco stood at the center of the group, Mary Lynn not far from his side. Although they were together, there seemed to be a distance between them. "One adult on each team. No more than three basketball players on a team."

"We've got three," Hubie Brown yelled, slinging his beefy right arm around Bryan's shoulders and draping his left over Frankie Polkowski, another starter.

"As I was saying before the interruption," Tony said, which got a big laugh from the rest of the team, "we'll play a round-robin format with the winners of the first two games meeting in the championship. So let's form the teams."

"We get Keri," Garrett Patterson yelled.

"Hey, she's my mom," Bryan protested.

"I called her first." Garrett crowed as though he'd won top prize in a lottery. "You're okay with it, right, Keri?"

"As long as Rose and I are a package deal." Keri moved a step closer to Rose, who seemed both nervous and pleased.

Murmurs arose from a few of the boys, but all Garrett said was "Cool."

"Then we get Coach," Frankie Polkowski said. No surprise there. Frankie was the friendliest player on the team and the one who tried hardest to stay on Grady's good side. Bryan shot his teammate a withering look, which Frankie seemed not to notice. "But here's the deal. Hold up your end or we'll make you run suicides."

Even Bryan laughed.

After Tony assigned the first-round matchups, a Bowl-arama employee briefed the players about how to use the laser tag equipment. It was fairly simple. Hit the red or blue lights on an opposing team member's vest with the infrared beam emitting from your phaser, and you racked up points for your side.

Grady's team was up first against six players that included Sid Humphries, the junior varsity coach. Sid didn't say much while acting as Grady's assistant during varsity games but yelled "I'm hit!" every time an opposing player nailed him.

The rest of the players moved stealthily through the

swirling fog in the darkened arena, but not Sid. His cries rang out over the theme music from James Bond movies, allowing the opposition to find him again and again.

"You'd think a young guy like you would be better at laser tag," Grady remarked to Sid after the game.

"You'd think." Sid laughed, unbothered by his team's ignominious defeat. Beads of sweat glistened at his hairline. "C'mon. I'll buy you a bottle of water while you wait to see who you face in the championship game."

Grady waited, his mouth talking basketball, his eyes on the entrance to the laser tag arena, his mind on how Rose was handling her sports prosthesis. Running was prohibited, but laser tag required crouching behind walls and moving quickly from point to point.

He didn't relax until he spotted the grin on Rose's face when she emerged from the arena. Keri followed, looking equally happy. Rose told Keri something, then veered off in the direction of the lanes while Keri walked toward the snack bar.

"How'd you do, Keri?" Sid called, drawing her attention. Her steps faltered when she saw Sid wasn't alone, but she continued to the counter where they sat side by side.

"We slaughtered 'em," Keri said.

"Watch out in the next game, Coach," Sid told Grady. "Sounds like she's out for blood."

Sid excused himself to keep a date with a Springhill player who'd challenged him to a video game showdown. Keri grabbed a bottled water from the refrigerated case beside the cash register and paid for her purchase.

Before she could retreat, Grady asked, "How'd Rose do?"

"Better than I hoped." Her eyes sparkled, and she

seemed to forget the awkwardness between them. "You should have seen her in there, Grady. She was having fun. She wasn't even thinking about her leg."

That mushrooming confidence in the prosthesis hadn't come easily. Rose had worked hard over the past few weeks, learning how to treat the prosthesis as an extension of herself rather than an artificial limb.

"Where is Rose?" he asked.

"Hanging out with some kids from school. She's meeting me here in a few minutes."

"So she's making friends?"

Keri sat down on the stool next to him. "Thanks to you."

"Me?" He pointed to his chest, genuinely puzzled by her comment. "What did I do?"

"You're kidding me, right?" She swiveled her stool so it was angled in his direction. "What you said about sports building self-esteem, it's true. And Rose isn't even on the track team yet."

"She will be." Grady spotted Rose rushing up to the counter, moving as effortlessly as any other teenage girl. "Speaking of the star now, here she comes."

"Your team's going down, Grady." Rose pointed to the ground and made her eyes bug out comically. "Prepare to lose."

"Not so fast," Grady said. "We beat that other team pretty badly."

"That team didn't have a secret weapon like we do," Rose said with a touch of smugness.

Grady made a disbelieving sound. "What secret weapon?"

"Keri." She threw up both of her hands as though the

answer was obvious. "Garrett didn't pick her first for nothing. She's a ringer."

"I didn't know there were such things as ringers in laser tag," Grady said.

"Oh, yeah," Rose answered with an air of authority. "Keri grew up near a laser tag place. She used to play all the time."

"It's true. I rule at laser tag," Keri said, but Grady could almost see the tongue in her cheek.

"Nobody wins all the time," he said.

Keri raised a skeptical eyebrow. "Have you seen who's on your team?"

"Some pretty good athletes."

"Some pretty *big* athletes. Bryan's six-five, Hubie and Frankie are almost as tall, and you're, what, six-four? Awfully big targets."

He tapped his chin, conceding her point. But she was forgetting something. "My big guys have quick reflexes. I'm picking us to take home the gold."

"Wanna bet?" Keri asked lightly.

"Hey, you should bet." Rose latched on to Keri's question, although Grady was fairly certain it was just one of those things people say. "Grady, if our team wins, you can buy Keri dinner."

Just Keri?

"And if your team wins," Rose continued smugly, "Keri can buy you dinner."

Grady no longer wondered why Rose hadn't included herself in the equation. He knew a setup when he saw one.

"Hey, Rose." A skinny blond girl who looked a lot like Garrett Patterson ran up to them. She was out of breath and no more than seven years old. "My brother's looking for you. Something about talking *stragy*."

"Strategy," Rose corrected. She looked at Keri. "You coming?"

"You go ahead," Keri said. "I'll be there in a minute."

Rose nodded, then rushed off with Garrett's sister, her enthusiasm making her seem almost as young as the little girl.

"About the bet," Keri began.

Grady braced himself, knowing what was coming.

"I apologize for Rose. She doesn't realize there's a… history between us." Keri's chest rose and fell. "So we can just forget about it."

"Afraid you'll lose?" That wasn't what Grady had planned to say. He intended to let her back out of the bet, not to goad her.

She met his eyes. "I'm not afraid."

"Prove it. That date you canceled. If my team wins, it's back on."

Her brows drew together. "Why would you still want to go out with me?"

He held her gaze. "Maybe because if you got to know me better, you'd realize I'm not such a bad guy."

"What happens if my team wins?"

"I stop asking you out."

She didn't reply for the space of five heartbeats. He knew how many because he counted. Finally she stuck out her hand.

"Deal," she said.

WHAT HAD POSSESSED KERI to agree to such a ridiculous bet?

She wasn't a teenage boy who constantly needed to

prove something, no matter how silly. Yet she'd accepted a bet that rested on her skill at laser tag, of all things.

Her vest vibrated, and one of the eight red lights that served as targets for the opposing players briefly turned white. She'd been hit for the third time, the maximum number allowable before having to recharge her phaser.

If she didn't focus, she'd find herself on a date with Grady Quinlan.

Not allowing herself to analyze how she felt about that, she quickly moved through the fake fog toward the recharger. The playing area was on two levels, linked by a series of black ramps lined on both sides with walls of varying shapes and sizes.

She spotted red lights, signifying one of her team members. It was Rose, squatting down behind a low black wall. Catching Keri's eye, Rose pointed to the blue lights on the vest of an unsuspecting opposing player. Rose came out shooting, infrared lights emitting from her phaser.

The blue-team player—Keri thought it was Bryan—retreated behind another wall for cover. Rose smiled, her teeth a flash of white in the darkness.

"You're a natural," Keri called to her in a loud whisper. "I have to recharge. Cover me."

"Got it," Rose said.

This was dangerous territory. Smart players hung around an opponent's charging station, hoping to hit stationary targets. Keri hooked her phaser to the machine, waited until she heard the futuristic sound signaling her gun had recharged, then zigzagged to a hiding spot.

"Good job," she said to Rose, and caught another glimpse of white teeth.

"Five minutes to play," a disembodied voice called over the loudspeaker. "The blue team is ahead."

If the blue team won, Keri had a date with Grady. Remembering Grady's intent gaze as he outlined the terms of the bet, Keri's heart pumped faster than the beat of the James Bond music. She needed to focus on the game and not on Grady's admission that he still wanted to go out with her.

Or her growing belief that a man who was helping a handicapped girl was the right kind of man.

Blue lights appeared to her left. She recognized Hubie Brown, mostly because of his neon orange shirt. She aimed, fired and watched one of the blue lights turn white. She hadn't been joking when she claimed tall guys made big targets. She'd tagged Hubie, Bryan and Frankie at least three times each, although Grady proved elusive.

"One minute to go," the loudspeaker voice announced. "Teams are tied."

Moving silently through the arena, Keri managed not to get tagged even though the blue targets stayed well hidden.

"Fifteen seconds," the voice said. "It's a virtual deadlock. It's coming down to the wire. Ten, nine, eight…"

Blue lights appeared off to her right. Grady. She aimed her phaser, then noticed Rose hunkering behind a wall, her back to Grady. He was approaching from her blind side.

"Seven, six, five, four…"

Intending to tag Grady before he got to Rose, Keri started to squeeze the trigger. But then Grady brought his hand to his mouth, as though he was…coughing? On purpose?

"Four, three…"

Keri's finger stilled. Rose whirled, aimed her phaser and got Grady square in the chest.

"Two, one. The red team wins!"

"I tagged you," Rose cried in delight.

Grady held up his hands in surrender. "You were too good for me."

Rose hurried off to join Garrett and the other members of the red team in a victory dance. Keri hung back, approaching Grady, as the other players filed out of the arena.

"You had a clear shot at Rose and you didn't take it," she said in a soft voice.

"You saw that, did you? I couldn't bring myself to tag her." She could make out his grimace in the semidarkness. "Although right about now, looking at you, I'm wishing I'd gone for the victory."

"I'm glad you didn't," she said.

He winced. "I get the message. Loud and clear."

"That didn't come out right. I meant…" Keri stopped, at a loss as to how to explain herself. His expression looked pinched, almost pained. She'd done that to him, and he didn't deserve it.

She kissed him.

Not on the chin. Not on the cheek. Right on the mouth. Without warning. Even without much conscious thought.

One moment she was standing an arm's length away. The next she was moving forward, anchoring her hands on his shoulders, standing on tiptoe and laying one on him.

He tasted even better than she imagined he would. Warm and male and intoxicating. His mouth, firm at first, softened almost immediately, molding to hers as if they'd kissed a hundred times instead of just this once.

She moved one of her hands from his shoulder to his lean cheek, which felt slightly stubbly beneath her fingertips. His lips parted, and she continued as the aggressor, her tongue venturing forward, touching his tongue, stroking it, closing her eyes at the sheer pleasure of kissing him.

He let her lead, not crushing her into his arms as some guys would have done, but taking only as much as she was willing to give. Shock coursed through her as she realized she was willing to give a great deal.

Gathering her weakening resolve, she managed to pull back from his soft, sexy mouth. The Bond music had stopped, and all she heard was the unevenness of her breathing. And his. Neither of them said anything for long moments.

Keri eventually broke the silence. "About that bet. Would it be okay if we changed it?"

"Changed it how?"

She wet her well-kissed lips. "My team won so it only seems fair you should buy me dinner."

His smile started slow and grew, all traces of disappointment on his lean, attractive face gone. And for the first time since the game ended, Keri felt as though she'd truly emerged on the winning side.

CHAPTER TEN

THE SOUND OF THE DOORBELL resounded through the quiet house on Sunday afternoon, spurring Keri into action.

She jumped up from the kitchen chair where she'd been reading the same newspaper paragraph in the thick Sunday paper over and over and dashed for the door, almost tripping over the pair of snow boots somebody had left in the front hall.

"Don't run," she told herself, then clamped a hand over her mouth to stifle a giggle.

She felt like a teenager about to go on her first date. Since she hadn't been out with a man since taking custody of the kids, this almost qualified as her first. She was certain of one thing. She'd never looked forward to a date more, especially after that kiss last night.

Grady had phoned an hour ago from the health club to go over the arrangements. After the mother of Rose's new friend, Rachel, picked Rose up at the club, Grady would swing by the house to get Keri. He'd told her to dress casually. He hadn't told her where he was taking her.

She flung open the door to Tony Marco. She felt her smile disappear.

"What are you doing here?" she asked.

He put a hand over his heart. "Is that any way to greet a friend?"

She didn't let his wounded tone affect her. "I asked what you're doing here, Tony."

He let his hand drop. "You won't return my calls. What else could I do?"

"Be a grown-up and accept we don't have anything to talk about." She started to shut the door.

He wrapped his hand around the edge of the door frame. "I wouldn't be here if that was true."

Momentum was with her, but memories of how she'd once felt about him stopped her from shutting the door the rest of the way and crushing his fingers.

"Fine." She stepped back, making it implicit that she was letting him into the house. "Now talk."

He shut the door behind him, and she immediately felt claustrophobic.

"Where are Bryan and Rose?" he asked.

She debated about whether to admit they weren't home, then figured he'd be more likely to state his business and go if he knew the truth. "Out."

He accepted her answer in silence, shrugged from his jacket and held it out. She didn't take it. Bella appeared at her side, the cat uncharacteristically rubbing against her leg, as though lending support.

"C'mon, Keri. Can't we at least sit down?" he asked.

"You won't be here that long," she said.

He stroked his mustache. "You didn't used to be this hard."

"I've changed. Lots of things have changed." She crossed her arms over her midsection. "What do you want, Tony?"

"You're not going to make this easy on me, are you?"

"No, I'm not. So just say what you need to say and go."

"I've been thinking about the past a lot, about the mistakes I made with you." His sigh was audible. His Adam's apple bobbed. "I was a jerk, Keri. I should never have given you an ultimatum when you took guardianship of Bryan and Rose."

She'd half forgiven him years ago. It had been on an ordinary night in the middle of winter when she gazed at her children and understood the true meaning of love. She knew what she'd felt for Tony paled in comparison, which must have been why she'd resisted setting a wedding date. No matter how difficult it was to raise two kids alone, she knew then that she'd choose Bryan and Rose all over again.

The visible regret in Tony's eyes caused the vestiges of resentment Keri had been harboring to fade to nothing. She opened her mouth to forgive him, but he spoke first.

"I never should have let you go, Keri," he said.

Her mouth dropped the rest of the way open, no words emerging. Although Tony had been showing signs of interest for months, she hadn't anticipated it would come to this. Tony was a decent man. She wouldn't have been engaged to him if he wasn't.

"You don't mean that," she said. "What about Mary Lynn?"

An emotion she couldn't identify flickered across his face. Guilt? Regret? Love? "Mary Lynn and I are having problems."

Same old Tony, she thought. When the going got tough, Tony bailed out. "Then work them out," she said.

He swept a hand through his thick, dark hair, a gesture

she remembered meant he was troubled. "Do you know how hard it is to be married to a woman who's set on having a baby? Especially when she's not getting pregnant?"

Keri shook her head from side to side. "You shouldn't be talking to me about this, Tony."

"Why not? We used to talk about everything."

"That was before you got married."

"Yeah, well, maybe I shouldn't have gotten married. Don't you remember how good things used to be between us?"

"Used to be," she said firmly. "I've moved on."

"To what?" Something seemed to occur to him. "Another man?"

She thought of Grady and how eagerly she'd been anticipating his arrival. "That's none of your business."

His eyes flicked over her, as though he were noticing what she was wearing for the first time. She'd had a hard time deciding, considering and rejecting a number of outfits. She'd settled on a pretty burgundy sweater that always earned her compliments and a flattering pair of jeans that looked better with the high-heeled half boots she'd already put on. "Is that why you keep looking toward the door? Are you expecting him?"

If she'd been casting glances at the door, it was in the hopes that Tony would be gone when Grady arrived. "Again. None of your business."

His eyes narrowed. "Is it my cousin?"

She said nothing, although she wasn't surprised at his guess. Mary Lynn hadn't let Tony out of her sight last night at the bowling alley, but Keri had felt Tony's eyes following her every move.

"Damn it all to hell," Tony said. "It *is* Grady. I'm surprised somebody as self-righteous as you would go out with him."

Keri felt her back stiffen. "If you're talking about what happened at Carolina State, I know all about it."

"I doubt that," Tony said with a harsh laugh. "What did he tell you? That he didn't do it? That it was all a big misunderstanding?"

He hadn't told her anything, Keri realized, but she wasn't about to share that information with Tony. "I want you to leave, Tony."

"Because of Grady?"

"Because you made a mistake in coming here and talking to me like this," she said. "We were over a long time ago. You know it as well as I do."

"But—"

"Go home to your wife, Tony. She doesn't deserve this. And you haven't done anything yet that you can't put right."

He stared at her for several minutes before his shoulders drooped, giving her hope that she'd actually gotten through to him. He pulled his jacket back on and let himself out into the cold.

She closed the door behind him, feeling as though a phase of her life had truly and irrevocably ended. She exhaled slowly, letting the tension leave her. Then she checked her watch, confirming that Grady was due at any moment. Her heart felt lighter, as though already open to new possibilities.

THE TWO-LANE ROAD, made narrower by the plowed piles of snow that bracketed both sides, reminded Grady of a roller coaster track. It snaked up and down hills, wound around curves and required the operator of the car to be alert. Grady had driven the route once before but couldn't afford to take his eyes off the road.

That was both a bad and a good thing. Bad because he couldn't gaze his fill at Keri, who looked fresh faced and lovely. Good because he wanted to sound casual when he broached the subject uppermost on his mind.

"I saw Tony coming out of your house," he said.

He couldn't afford more than a glance at her, but he still had an impression of white around her irises.

"It's not what you think," she said.

He thought she might need him to tell Tony to leave her alone. "What do I think?"

"That I'm involved with Tony. That I'm somehow encouraging him." She sounded distressed.

"You're not." He maneuvered the car around a curve. The road opened into a snow-covered valley dotted with evergreen trees, but he was too preoccupied to appreciate the scenery.

"How can you be so sure?" she asked.

"Are you trying to tell me you *are* involved with Tony?"

"No!" she exclaimed heatedly.

He slanted her a quick smile. "I was joking. I know your problems with Tony stem from Tony."

"But how do you know that?"

The quick answer was that he just knew, but her question forced him to examine his reasons. "You're uncomfortable around him. But even if you weren't, I know you wouldn't fool around with a married man."

She released an audible breath. "I wish Mary Lynn had

as much faith in me as you. She thinks I've got something going with her husband."

"I'm not so sure about that," he said slowly, careful not to break Mary Lynn's confidence about her fertility problems. "But I do think she considers you a threat."

"I'm no threat," Keri protested. "I wouldn't date Tony even if he were single."

Every protective instinct Grady possessed rose up inside him. Not only for Keri, but for Mary Lynn. "Want me to tell Tony that for you?"

"I told him myself. Just before you picked me up. Not in those words, exactly. But it seemed like he finally got the message." She was silent as she fiddled with her gloves. "He told me he and Mary Lynn are having trouble conceiving."

Grady said nothing.

"I've heard that can put a real strain on a marriage," Keri said. "That must be why Tony is acting so, I don't know, out of character."

"When did he start bothering you?"

"Just these past three or four months. Now I think it has something to do with Mary Lynn not getting pregnant."

"Could be," Grady said, although his cousin had never said anything to him about wanting children. Then again, he and Tony weren't close.

"Enough about Tony," Keri said, finality in her voice. "Where are you taking me?"

"It's a surprise." He spotted his turnoff past a tall evergreen on the right side of the road.

"Are we almost there?" she asked.

He slowed the car and pulled over, thankful the plows

had pushed the snow to the very edge of the wide shoulder, allowing them to park safely.

"We *are* there," Grady said.

He enjoyed the confusion that furrowed her brows as she studied the nothingness around them.

"Grady Quinlan," she said, one fist perched on her hip, mock censure in her voice. "Did you bring me up here to park?"

He shouted with laughter, then cupped the back of her head and gave her a swift kiss on her lips.

"Not a bad idea," he said. An understatement considering the temperature of his blood was elevating even though he'd shut off the heater. "But not the right guess."

Her fingers went to her lips, as though she'd been as affected by the brief contact as he. "Then why are we here?"

He lifted the latch that popped the trunk.

"Get out of the car and I'll show you."

She followed his lead, her pretty mouth curved in bemusement as she accompanied him to the back of the car. "I swear, Grady," she muttered. "If there's a dead body in there…"

He laughed again, reached into the trunk and pulled out a large piece of molded purple plastic.

"A sled!" she exclaimed. "You brought me here to sled?"

"Another teacher told me about this place. I checked it out the other day. Almost nobody knows about it."

She gazed down at her jeans and her brown leather shoe boots, which were designed more for fashion than functionality. "How am I going to sled wearing this?"

He held up a finger, then pulled blue snow pants, a matching ski jacket, a sturdy pair of snow boots, mittens and a knit hat from the trunk.

"Those are mine!" she said. "How did you get them?"

"I had some help from my, uh, accomplice."

"Your accomplice?" Her voice rose on the word. "You mean Rose?"

"Yeah," Grady said. "She asked where I was taking you, then offered to sneak into your room and get your stuff."

"You talked to Rose about us?"

He liked that Keri thought there was an us. "Rose talked to *me*. She says you need to have more fun."

"She does, does she?"

"Yep." He lifted the other sled from the trunk. It was purple like the first one, the only color the store had in stock. "She says you're pretty old and creaky but you should still have fun."

"She called me creaky?" She sounded outraged. Comically so.

"I embellished," he admitted. "But I think she's right."

"That I'm old and creaky?"

He laughed. "That you should have more fun. So put on those snow pants and boots and let's get started."

KERI TRAIPSED HAPPILY through the snow, pulling her purple sled behind her up the hill, feeling pleasantly warm despite the cool wind spraying powdery snow into the air.

She reached the summit, enjoying the wintry scene. Snow clung to the branches of the evergreens in the distance and coated their sled hill, pristine except for the paths their two sleds had made.

"Ready for another go?" Grady asked, already in position. Instead of situating her sled next to Grady's, as she had the last three or four times they'd sped downhill in tandem, she let go of the pull rope and left the sled where it lay.

"Move over," she told Grady, plopping down on the sled in front of him. She turned her head to enjoy the surprised look on his face. "I think it's time we doubled up."

"Are you sure?" He was hatless and particles of snow clung to his brown hair, hinting at the distinguished way he'd look when he started to gray. "With our combined weight, the sled's gonna fly down the hill."

"Why do you think I suggested it?" She made her eyebrows dance. "I'm tired of you going faster than me."

"Then hold on," he said, his breath warm against her cheek. He rocked the sled, then used his feet to push along the snow.

Keri lifted her feet onto the purple plastic, and Grady's strong arms wrapped securely around her midsection. The sled gathered momentum as it skimmed over the snow, the wind whipping at their faces. She felt cold air against her teeth and realized she was smiling and that there was nowhere she'd rather be than on this sled with this man.

From her previous trips she anticipated the slight bump halfway down the hill but didn't foresee the sled going airborne.

She shouted as her stomach seemed to leap into her throat. This, she thought, must be what it was like to fly.

The sled seemed to hang suspended in the air before it hit the ground once again, tottering before leveling out and sliding safely to the bottom of the hill.

Grady's arms loosened and Keri turned to face him, kneeling on the sled in front of him so she straddled his lap. "That was fantastic!"

He grinned at her. "You weren't afraid we'd wipe out?"

"Nope." The thought hadn't entered her mind. Not once. Not when Grady had her enfolded in his arms. "I was born to fly through the air on a sled."

Grady laughed, his smile as wide as the snow stretching around them in every direction.

She couldn't be sure later who moved toward whom, but suddenly they were kissing. His cool lips slid against her own, his warm breath mingled with hers, the white snow around them fading to black because he was the only thing she could see.

She'd remember this kiss, she thought dazedly, for a very long time. Maybe even for the rest of her life.

After what could have been an eternity or possibly only seconds, they drew back.

Joy filled her, as bright as the winter sky. She got to her feet and grinned down at him.

"Let's do it again!"

After more wild trips down the sled hill, they finally called it a day, stopping at a coffee shop on the way back to Springhill. Keri cupped her steaming mug of hot chocolate with both hands, letting the warmth seep into her skin, but she could still feel the sting of cold on her cheeks.

She'd seldom felt more alive than she did today.

Grady sat in his seat with his own cup of hot chocolate and grinned at her. Windburn lent his skin a slight tinge of red, his eyes were bright and his thick hair as deliciously messy as she'd ever seen it.

"You are hell on a sled," he said.

She chuckled. "Thanks for taking me. I can't remember when I've had so much fun."

"I needed some fun, too." He scooted his chair nearer their table for two, put down the mug and leaned closer to her. "Look into my eyes and tell me what you see."

He had beautiful eyes, oval shaped, wide spaced and a shade of hazel she didn't see often. "Little black dots in the middle of your irises," she joked.

"No tiny basketball players?"

"None."

"Good. I was afraid they were embedded on my pupils after all the game film I've been watching."

She laughed. "You want to win that badly?"

"I want to prepare my players to do their best."

"That's the same thing," Keri said.

He shook his head. "Not in my book. Winning's nice, sure. But it's not as important as competing well."

She thought over what she knew about Grady's coaching style. Unlike some high school coaches who played only their top seven or eight guys, Grady made sure his weaker players got into almost every game for at least a few minutes.

Keri tapped the table with the tips of her fingers. "Remember that game where Joey Jividen missed an easy layup when time was running out?"

He nodded once. "Sure do."

"When you got the ball back, why did you let Joey take the last shot of the game?"

Grady didn't hesitate before replying, "I didn't want him to think of himself as a failure."

"But what if he'd missed again?"

"Unlikely. Kids generally respond pretty well when you show you believe in them."

"But what if Joey *had* missed?" she persisted, eager to gain insight into how his brain worked.

"I'd have put him in another position to succeed," he said. "If not in the next game, then in the game after that."

"That's—" she groped for a word "—amazing."

He squirmed in his seat, the praise seeming to make him uncomfortable. "Not really. Joey's a pretty good player."

"I didn't mean Joey. I meant your philosophy." It didn't jibe with what had reportedly gone down at Carolina State, yet Tony had alluded to Grady's guilt scant hours ago. Had the scandal caused Grady to reevaluate his approach to coaching? Would he talk about it or was it something better left in the past?

"A lot of people don't agree with my philosophy," Grady said before she discovered whether she had the nerve to bring up Carolina State. "Some of my players don't."

Her mind shifted gears. Bryan had complained enough about Grady that she got the reference. "You're talking about Bryan."

"He's one of them."

Bryan's major complaint was that Grady didn't play him enough. A regulation high school basketball game consisted of four eight-minute quarters. Bryan typically played twenty-four of those thirty-two minutes, a decent amount but markedly less than star players on other teams.

"Look at it from Bryan's point of view," Keri said. "His goal is to play college ball so he wants to impress the scouts by having a high scoring average. The more he plays, the more he scores."

"Last I looked, he was averaging twenty points per game."

Keri didn't pay attention to scoring averages, but she did listen to Bryan. "He says he could be averaging more."

"True," Grady said. "But if Bryan played more, some of his teammates wouldn't play at all."

At the implied criticism, she felt her stomach tighten. "Are you saying Bryan's a bad teammate?"

"Not at all. He'll pass up a shot if he can get a teammate a better one."

"Then what are you saying?"

"With Bryan, it's me first."

"You just said he gets a lot of assists," she refuted. "Doesn't that prove he puts the team first?"

"It proves he wants to win. And that he knows college scouts value a good pass almost as much as a good shot."

She shook her head in disbelief. "Why can't you give him the benefit of the doubt about anything?"

He didn't answer quickly. "Maybe because he reminds me of somebody I used to know."

"It must not have been somebody you liked. I wish you'd look past what you think you know about him and really see him. He's a good kid, Grady." She'd said that so many times Grady was probably starting to wonder if she was trying to convince herself.

"I never said he wasn't," Grady said.

"But you…" Keri let her voice trail off and took a deep breath to calm herself. Until they started talking about Bryan, they'd had a wonderful day. She didn't want it to end in acrimony. "Can we change the subject? Agree to disagree?"

"Love to," he said. "Let's talk about that dinner I owe you."

"Didn't you take me sledding in lieu of buying me dinner?"

"Nope. The bet was for dinner. So how about we go to Suzette's next Saturday night?" He named the finest restaurant in Springhill.

She bit her bottom lip, wondering how to tactfully refuse. "Could we go somewhere else?"

"Sure," he said. "I hear Coscarelli's Italian Grill is good, too. How about there?"

"Somewhere not in Springhill." She couldn't not explain what was on her mind now. "We live in a small town, Grady. I'm not ready for people to know we're dating yet."

He crossed his arms over his chest. "Does this have anything to do with Bryan?"

"In a way. He knows we've been out a few times, and he's dealing with it. It'd be harder on him if all his friends know, too." When he said nothing, she continued, "Please try to understand. I'm his mom. You're his basketball coach. Even if you two didn't have issues, it's a difficult situation."

"You're right." He reached across the table to take her hand, his expression softening. "Then let's make it as easy as possible. I don't care where we have dinner, as long as we have it together."

She nodded, feeling the corners of her lips lift. "You're an amazing man."

"I wondered when you'd realize that." He winked at her.

She laughed, but his self-deprecating wink only solidified her impression. He truly was amazing.

TEN MINUTES BEFORE the free-throw contest and still no Jackie Fitzgibbons.

Bryan had reminded her about the contest in school on Friday, telling her to be sure to bring her little brother, although they both knew Bryan was much more interested in seeing Jackie show up.

He finished autographing a basketball for a towheaded kid who said he was eight years old and never missed a Springhill game.

"There you go, Donny." Bryan ruffled the boy's hair. "Come say hi when you see me around."

"Thanks," the boy said breathlessly, dimples flashing, eyes worshipping.

Donny ran off, yelling to anyone who would listen that he'd gotten Bryan Charleton's autograph. Bryan did another visual sweep of the gym and again failed to spot Jackie.

"Great season you're having." The voice belonged to Mario Adamski, the pizza parlor owner who treated Bryan to free food after big games. "Keep it up."

"I'll try my best, Mr. Adamski," Bryan said.

Mr. Adamski gestured to the three or four dozen kids taking turns heaving practice shots at the six baskets in the Grace School. Bryan and Reverend Martin had lowered the side hoops from ten feet to eight for the younger kids, but a lot of them still had trouble sinking the shots.

"Good turnout you've got here," Mr. Adamski said.

"Not too shabby," Bryan agreed as his attention was snagged by a dark-haired boy of about eight or nine with skinny legs extending from bright green shorts. He used a baseball pitcher's motion to hurl the ball at the hoop. It kept coming up a good six feet short. An overhead light caught the glisten of tears on the boy's cheek.

"Excuse me, Mr. Adamski." Bryan jogged over to the boy to find silent fat tears dripping down his round cheeks. Bryan got down on his haunches so they were at eye level. "Hey, bud. What's your name?"

The boy sniffed loudly. "Trey."

"You've never shot a free throw before, have you, Trey?"

Trey's thin chest expanded, then contracted on a shuddering breath. "No."

"The first time I tried, all I hit was air, too."

"Really?"

"Really. I didn't make one till someone showed me the right way to shoot."

Trey blinked a few times, drying up the tears pooling in his dark eyes. "There's a right way?"

"Sure is." Bryan gestured toward the least-crowded basket. "Let's go over there and I'll show you."

Five minutes of instruction later, Trey still couldn't sink a shot but could at least hit the rim. Bryan wasn't sure which one of them was more nervous when it came time for his turn at the line.

"Come on, Trey. You can do it, bud," Bryan said, then pumped his fist for encouragement.

His tongue protruding from between his lips, Trey stepped to the line and went into his new improved motion.

The first shot was wide left. The next eight missed in a variety of ways—wide left, short, long, wide right—until Trey was oh of nine.

"You're close." Bryan kept up his constant encouragement so the boy's tears wouldn't start flowing again. "Just remember what I told you and make this one count."

Trey lined up his last shot.

"Use the guide hand, bend your knees, extend," Bryan whispered under his breath as the boy went through the motion.

The ball arced into the air and dropped straight through the hoop.

"I did it! I did it!" Trey jumped up and down as if he'd just won the NBA finals.

"Yes!" Bryan yelled, running to the line to slap palms.

The rest of the afternoon passed in a blur of kids taking free throws, although nobody else got as excited as Trey had for going one of ten from the line.

Finally, after Bryan chased down what felt like missed shot number one thousand, the contest was over.

He was helping Keisha round up the basketballs when somebody tapped him on the shoulder. It barely registered that the shoulder-tapper was Jackie Fitzgibbons before she opened his hand and pressed a piece of paper into it. On it was a string of ten numbers.

"I don't understand," he said. "Why'd you change your mind?"

"You changed it for me," she said mysteriously.

She left him and joined a woman across the gym who looked like an older version of herself. With them was a boy still vibrating with excitement.

Trey.

The woman took one of Trey's hands and Jackie took the other. Trey launched himself into the air, his legs jack-knifing.

Jackie, it seemed, had showed up to watch her brother after all.

CHAPTER ELEVEN

THE ONLY OCCUPANT OF THE break room where the Springhill High teachers congregated during free periods glared at Grady with open disdain.

That didn't happen to Grady often now that his basketball team was 22-1 and cruising through the district playoffs. Nobody expected anything less than a victory tonight in the district championship game.

That included Grady, although he'd never say so aloud. He still thought anything could happen on any given night, but defeat was unlikely against an opponent that hadn't gotten within twenty points of Springhill the last two times they played.

He crossed the room to the coffeepot and said as pleasantly as he could, "Good morning, Mrs. Winchell."

She grunted, then lowered her gray head to the newspaper spread out in front of her on the table. Eleanor Winchell had been teaching math classes at Springhill High for thirty years with a passion that had won her numerous Teacher of the Year awards. Grady knew that because her trophies were displayed in a glass case by the main office. Grady had heard that students either loved her or hated her, depending on how hard they were willing to work in her class.

He poured himself a cup of coffee, which he took black, then sipped it while standing at the counter. If it had been any other teacher, he would have asked if he could join her or him.

"I hear we're in for a thaw," he said, figuring snowmelt to be a safe topic of discussion.

She looked up at him over the rim of her glasses, her eyebrows crinkling in the centers so they resembled inverted *V*s. "Isn't that interesting?"

It was the most she'd ever said to him. Her eyes lowered again, dismissing him. But why? What had he done to make her act like this toward him? There was only one way to find out.

"Do you have a problem with me, Mrs. Winchell?"

She lowered her newspaper, straightened her back and looked him full in the face. "Yes, as a matter of fact, I do have a problem with you."

"What is it?"

She snorted. "As though someone like you would care what I think."

He did care what people thought of him, he realized. That had always been his problem.

"Try me," he said.

"Okay. I find it abhorrent, Mr. Quinlan, that you have continued the shameful tradition this school has of giving preferential treatment to basketball players." She seemed to gain steam as she talked. "It is morally reprehensible for you to foster the idea that athletics are more important than education."

"I don't believe that," he protested.

"Oh, please, Mr. Quinlan. Next you'll claim to be

unaware that teachers in this school give Bryan Charleton passing grades even when he's failing."

Grady processed the information, discovering he could easily believe it. "You know that for a fact?"

"I know Bryan managed to transfer out of my class after his first F. I know he can barely add, yet somehow he's getting B's in Jack Patterson's Algebra Two class. And I know he's getting B's because I checked his transcript."

Jack Patterson's son Garrett was the Cougars' point guard. Jack never missed a Springhill basketball game.

"I don't care if Bryan's the second coming of LeBron James," she began.

"You know who LeBron James is?" Grady asked.

"I have been known to watch a basketball game or two," she said with the same haughty air. "As I was saying, I don't care how good Bryan is, an educational institution should not teach him that education is unimportant."

Amen.

Grady dumped the rest of his coffee down the drain and headed for the exit, calling over his shoulder, "Excuse me, Ms. Winchell."

"There's no excuse," she began, but Grady heard no more.

The halls were deserted, as they usually were when class was in session. Grady's basketball shoes squeaked slightly on the tile floor as he hurried toward the west wing where most of the math classes were taught.

He didn't hesitate when he reached Jack Patterson's classroom. He pulled open the door and stuck in his head. Jack, who was perched on the edge of the desk, turned to him in surprise. So did all eyes in the room—including Bryan Charleton's.

It sunk in for the first time that this might not be the best time to talk to Jack, but it was too late. Besides, what Grady had to say was more important than any equation. "Mr. Patterson, could I have a minute?"

"Well, sure." Jack got up from the desk, talking to his class as he moved toward the door. "Here's a chance to get a jump start on your homework. Problems seven through fifteen in chapter eight."

Jack stepped into the hall, shutting the door behind him. He was a tidy, compact man who looked as if he still worked out regularly. Like his son, he wasn't much taller than five-eight. Grady wondered if Jack had played point guard in high school, too. "What is it, Grady?"

"It's about Bryan." There was no point in delaying what Grady wanted—no, needed—to know. "I heard you're changing his grades."

"What! Where'd you get that idea?" Jack appeared shocked, but Grady got the impression he was putting on an act. Maybe he'd been a drama student in high school, too.

"From another teacher."

"Has Mrs. Winchell been bad-mouthing me again?" Jack shook his head. "I swear, that woman can't mind her own business."

"Are you giving Bryan grades he doesn't deserve or aren't you?"

Jack didn't answer right away. "You've got Bryan in one of your own classes, Grady. You know he's not the strongest student around."

"Then it's true," Grady said, feeling sick to his stomach.

"What are you getting so upset about? The district final is tonight. Bryan can't play if he's academically ineligible."

"Damn it, Jack." Grady clenched his fists in frustration. "This isn't about basketball. It's about Bryan's education. If he's failing your class, give him a failing grade."

Jack's expression changed, the friendliness wiped out as surely as if somebody had taken an eraser to a chalkboard. "I never said Bryan was failing."

"You implied it."

"You misunderstood." His words sounded clipped, as if they'd been programmed into a robot. "Bryan's doing fine. Now, if you'll excuse me, I've got to be getting back to my class."

Grady stood in the hall, feeling powerless. He couldn't very well follow Jack Patterson into algebra class and accuse him of lying. But how could he right this terrible wrong when he had no way to prove Jack was granting Bryan special favors?

He needed to tell Keri. As Bryan's mother, she should know what was going on. Once she knew the extent of the problem, surely she'd try to rectify it.

But Keri hadn't believed in him once before. With no concrete proof, would Keri believe him now?

STEAMED VEGETABLES, mashed potatoes and grilled chicken topped with bacon, cheese and what smelled to Keri like honey mustard sauce filled the plates on the table set for two.

But the extra touches—the bowls of Caesar salad and chunks of crusty bread—sent guilt skittering through Keri.

"I have a confession to make," she blurted out.

Grady gazed at her from the linoleum countertop in his cozy kitchen, from where he'd just popped the cork on a bottle of cabernet sauvignon. "Can it wait until we sit down to eat?"

"No," she said. "I have to tell you now."

He left the wine unpoured, the glasses empty, and crossed to where she stood at the foot of the kitchen table. "What is it?"

"I was completely out of line for suggesting we shouldn't be seen in public together," she said in a rush. "I know what I said about our relationship being tough on Bryan, but I told him he just needs to deal."

"Well, that's…great." He obviously wasn't understanding her. "I thought it was going to be something bad."

"It is bad. I talked to Bryan about this days ago, but I'm only telling you now."

His face scrunched up. "What's so bad about that?"

"I was afraid you'd go back to the restaurant idea if I told you sooner. And I wanted it to be just the two of us."

"Let me get this straight," he said, one corner of his mouth heading north. "You're apologizing for wanting to be alone with me?"

She indicated the spread in front of them. "More for letting you go to all this trouble—"

"It wasn't that much trouble," he said.

"—when I'm the one who should be making you dinner."

"That wasn't the bet."

"Your team won districts last night." The Cougars had never trailed, winning by double digits to qualify for next week's regional tournament. "Tonight's dinner should be my treat."

His eyebrows waggled suggestively. "I can think of other ways you can treat me."

Keri laughed and let go of her guilt. She couldn't possibly hang on to it when he was making jokes like that.

"That'll teach me to make the first move on a guy," Keri muttered good-naturedly and walked into his arms. "Now you'll always expect me to kiss you first."

"For the record," he said as she twined her arms around his neck, "I don't care who makes the first move as long as one of us does."

His breath tickled her lips and she breathed in his now-familiar scent. Then she kissed him, experiencing that same indescribable high as she had the first time. As she probably would every time. She lost herself in the kiss, nothing more important than this moment and this man.

The years and the responsibility seemed to peel away until she was once again the woman she'd been before Maddy died. Somewhere between taking custody of the kids and dealing with Rose's medical problems, she'd lost her sense of self.

Until Grady.

Before he could deepen the kiss, she drew back in his arms and traced the contours of his sexy mouth. He couldn't know that his kiss affected her more than any other man's, that she didn't trust herself to be able to stop once they started. If she didn't put a halt to things now, the delicious dinner he'd prepared would grow cold.

"Aren't you going to feed me?" she asked.

His chest expanded and contracted. She felt, as much as heard, his sigh. "Do I have to?"

She laughed and pushed at his chest, disentangling from his arms. "I'm going to take full advantage of you tonight."

He growled playfully. "Promise?"

The meal continued in that same lighthearted vein while he entertained her with stories from what he called the PE trenches.

Such as the boy who fell flat on his face after his shorts, which he wore low on his hips, slipped to his ankles when the class was running laps. And the slight girl who demonstrated to the cocky quarterback that she could do more push-ups in a minute than him.

"I don't know what was better." Keri got up to clear the table when they were finished eating. "The stories or the food. You have to give me the recipe for that chicken dish."

"The recipe?" He looked confused. "Wait a minute. You don't think I cooked the food?"

"Didn't you?"

"Hell, no. I'm not a cook, but I'm an expert on every restaurant that offers takeout."

"But I thought…" Her voice trailed off. She hadn't thought deeply enough about the unlikelihood of a basketball coach who lived alone being able to cook like a professional chef. "I just saw the food and figured you'd cooked it."

"Hardly." He opened the cupboard under the sink and tossed some used napkins into a wastebasket full of foam take-out containers. "I can cook hot dogs and grilled cheese sandwiches, but that's about it."

The aluminum stovetop, in fact, showed no signs of recent activity. No splatters. No pots or pans that might have been used to prepare food.

"I feel like an idiot," she said.

"Don't. It was kind of flattering." A mischievous light entered his eyes. "Wait till you see what I did with dessert."

He opened the freezer portion of his refrigerator, reached inside and pulled out two ice cream sandwiches wrapped in white paper.

"Now, I know you didn't make those," Keri said.

He handed her one of the treats. "Wait for me beside the fireplace while I crush some more grapes for the wine."

"Ha, ha," she said, but she was laughing as she went into his living room. She'd expected Grady's home to be bigger, befitting his size, but he could probably get from one end to the other in ten strides. Yet somehow the coziness of the place, with its small rooms and the fireplace he'd set to blazing, suited him.

Classical music—Bach, another surprise—drifted through the house while she meandered over to the mantel above the fireplace. She picked up a framed photo of a beautiful, dark-haired woman in the arms of a man who looked like Grady.

"My parents," he told her, approaching from behind.

"Any brothers or sisters?"

"Only me."

"Where are your parents now?"

"My mom lives with my grandmother in a little town near Philadelphia called West Chester. My dad's a dispatcher for a trucking company in North Carolina."

Now the truck driving job made a little more sense. Grady's dad must have helped him secure it. "Your parents aren't together?"

"They divorced when I was five, remarried a few years later, then divorced for good when I was thirteen."

"Really?" She looked more closely at the photo but saw a couple who seemed very much in love instead of impending trouble. "Yet you still keep a photo of the two of them together."

"It reminds me of the good times," he said.

She put the photo back on the mantel and joined him on his comfortable navy-colored sofa. "Was the divorce tough on you?"

His shrug didn't fool her. "I had basketball."

She leaned her head back on the sofa cushion to gaze at him while her mind turned to another teenage boy who'd immersed himself in basketball when adversity struck. In Bryan's case, the ill fortune had been death instead of divorce. Bryan had poured his soul into the game then. She could easily envision Grady doing the same.

"Were you good?" she asked.

"Not as good as Bryan, but I did all right."

"Define 'all right.'"

"I had scholarship interest from some of the mid-majors," he said.

Keri had made it her business to become versed in Bryan's world so she was familiar with the term *mid-major.* It referred to schools with basketball programs a step down in size and prestige from notables such as Duke, Florida and Carolina State.

"But you played at Carolina State," she said. Almost all of the old newspaper stories about the scandal mentioned Grady had been a basketball player before being hired as an assistant coach.

"Not on scholarship. And I mostly sat the bench." He pointed to the side of her mouth. "You've got a piece of ice cream sandwich right there."

She brushed at the side of her mouth. "Did I get it?"

"No," he said. "Let me."

His lips replaced the spot where her fingers had been, and the edges of her mind went fuzzy. She sensed there was a story in why he'd ended up at Carolina State instead of playing basketball on scholarship elsewhere, but he was clearly trying to change the subject. At the moment she wasn't sure she cared.

"Was that a first move?" she asked.

"Nope. This is." He kissed her, his lips soft and inviting against her own. He tasted of the wine he'd drunk, and he seemed to go straight to her head. When she would have deepened the kiss, he slid his mouth from her lips to her cheek.

"Very nice move," she said.

"Wait until you see my second," he murmured.

The warmth from the fire—at least that might have been the source—touched every part of her body. "Don't tell me you're going to pull out a bearskin rug and lay it down in front of the fireplace."

"No way. We're not that kind of couple."

It sounded right when he referred to them as a unit. "What kind of couple are we?"

"This kind." In one swift move, he scooped her into his arms and stood up. She twined her arms tightly around his neck, although she had no fear he'd drop her.

"You think we're like Rhett Butler and Scarlett O'Hara?" she asked in a teasing voice that didn't match the furious racing of her heart.

"Nope. Those two were at each other's throats," he said, nuzzling hers.

"Richard Gere and Debra Winger?" she managed to

ask, her voice breathless. "Remember when he carried her out of the factory in *An Officer and a Gentleman?*"

"I won't be a gentleman where we're going." His breathing was vaguely ragged as he carried her through the house and down a hallway to a back bedroom, but she doubted the cause was exertion.

The only furniture in the room was a weathered wood dresser and a rather large bed, spartan even for a bachelor's bedroom.

"This is the guest room," he said.

Before she could ask why he'd brought her there, he laid her gently on the bed. And it rolled. "Oh, my gosh! I didn't think they made water beds like this anymore."

"The tenant before me left it. The newer models aren't as free flowing."

He got on the bed next to her, and she immediately tumbled into his arms. She laughed. "I like free flowing," she said as she molded herself against his length, feeling the unmistakable evidence that he wanted her.

She was still smiling when he kissed her, joy coursing through her along with the passion he could so easily unleash. She opened her mouth to him, their tongues tangled and the world rocked. Or maybe the rocking came from the bed that rolled and shifted with their every move, heightening every sensation.

She moved his hand from her waist to her breast, moaning against his mouth as he kneaded and teased until all she could think about was getting her clothes off. As though he'd read her mind, he reached under her sweater and she helped him unhook the front clasp of her bra. She tried to pull the garment over her head and elbowed him in the nose. He cried out.

"Sorry," she said.

"I can take the pain," he said, helping her pull the sweater the rest of the way off, "when you're the gain."

Keri had always yearned to be better endowed, but such appreciation gleamed in his eyes that she felt for the first time in her life she was perfect exactly the way she was.

He reached for her again, his mouth at her breast, one of his hands at the waistband of her jeans.

The water in the bed rolled like waves lapping the shore at high tide, impeding his progress, making it twice as difficult for Keri to wiggle out of her clothes.

"Damn bed doesn't want me to get you naked," he muttered, his impatience as arousing as it was humorous.

"We can't let a bed beat us," she said, and managed to pull off her jeans. Her underwear came off with them.

He tried to raise himself up on one elbow to look at her, but the bed wouldn't support him and he rolled into her. She embraced him, the feel of her nakedness sliding against the denim of his jeans and cotton of his shirt wonderfully erotic.

He kissed her again, long and hot, while his hand stroked her breast, then slid over her stomach to the juncture of her thighs. She cried out against his mouth when he touched her and found her wet and wanting.

"Not yet," she said, already feeling the excitement build inside her. "I want you naked, too."

In the next instant, he rolled away from her, not stopping until he was off the bed. He stood up with amazingly little difficulty and shed his clothes so fast it was as though somebody had challenged him to a race.

She barely had time to admire the width of his chest, the leanness of his hips and his very impressive erection before he joined her on the bed.

The bed rolled and pitched, and their bodies slammed into each other, the impact more shocking than painful.

"This mattress should come with a warning," he grumbled. "Make love at your own risk."

Even as the passion spiraled inside her and he sheathed himself with a condom he'd produced from somewhere, she laughed.

She opened her legs, wrapped them around his thighs and guided him inside her. Her laughter died at the sheer pleasure of being joined with him, but she felt herself smiling. They moved together, already seeming to know each other's rhythms. The bed made sloshing sounds as Grady redefined the meaning of what it meant to rock one's world.

And she knew as she spiraled toward climax that only one man would have suggested they make love for the first time in a water bed.

The man who was right for her.

KERI'S HEAD RESTED AGAINST Grady's shoulder, the sweet smell of her hair filling his nostrils as he watched the flames flicker in the fireplace. They'd made love twice, once in the water bed and again in his traditional bed. Both times, it felt as though his world had shifted, making room beside him for her.

"I need to get home soon," she said.

Rose was spending the night with a friend, but Bryan's curfew was midnight. "I know." He turned her in his arms so her very tempting mouth was just inches from his. "Which gives us at least another half hour."

"Oh, no." She turned her mouth so his kiss landed on her cheek instead of her lips. "You distracted me once. I won't let you do it again until you tell me why you didn't accept a scholarship at a mid-major."

He reluctantly let her go and stared at the orange-and-gold flames licking at the crackling wood in the fireplace. "It's not that interesting a story."

"I still want to hear it."

He sighed and turned to look at her. She'd seemed very pale the first time he saw her, but now color infused her skin and her green eyes glinted with what he recognized as determination.

"I never got offered any scholarships," he said. "I would have. But I tore my ACL in my senior season of high school."

"Your ACL? That's in your knee, right?"

"Right. The anterior cruciate ligament. It just snapped." He remembered the moment as though it happened yesterday. Leaping for a rebound in traffic and coming down with the ball. An opponent landing hard on the side of his knee. The feeling of something inside his knee popping, then a searing pain that went soul deep.

Sympathy filled Keri's eyes, as though she felt the pain, too. "Did you need surgery?"

"Oh, yeah. The ACL can't be repaired, only replaced." The injury had wiped out the rest of his senior season, the disappointment so crushing he felt it acutely even now. He'd been a good basketball player, but not a great one. Certainly not of the caliber to tempt a college coach to gamble on issuing him a coveted scholarship. "Rehab usually takes about six months after surgery, but I had complications. It took longer than that."

"But you played basketball at Carolina State," she said.

"Not right away. First I went to community college at a school near my dad's place in North Carolina. I transferred to Carolina State when I was a sophomore."

"What about basketball?"

"I kept working on my game, trying to get back to where I'd been. But I lost a step, which hurt because my game was built on speed."

"Yet you made the team at Carolina State," she stated, as though it were that simple.

"As a walk-on." He didn't bother explaining that walk-ons were nonscholarship players. With Bryan as a son, she'd know that already. "The team stars got more playing time in a single game than I got in my entire career."

She stroked his arm, compassion evident in her touch. "That must have been hard on you."

"Harder than it had to be," he said. There couldn't be a better opening to bring up the subject that had been at the back of his mind all evening. "That's one of the reasons I'm worried about Bryan."

"Bryan? I don't understand."

He slowly filled his lungs with oxygen while he thought about how to phrase his concerns. He exhaled. "I was counting on that athletic scholarship, the same way Bryan is. After the injury, my grades and SAT scores weren't good enough by themselves to get into any of the schools that recruited me."

She removed her hand from his arm. "Bryan's grades are fine."

Here goes, he thought. "Only because some of his teachers are changing them."

Faint horizontal lines creased her forehead. "Changing them?"

"From D's and F's to B's."

"What! Who?" She angled away from him so that no parts of their bodies touched.

"His algebra teacher, for starters."

"Jack Patterson? Garrett's dad." She sounded incredulous. "Jack told you this?"

Grady thought back over his conversation with Jack and answered truthfully. "He hinted at it, but when I tried to get him to admit it, he denied it."

She crossed her arms over her chest. Grady wasn't a body language expert but even he could tell she'd closed her mind to the possibility of grade fixing. "Then how do you know it's true?"

"Eleanor Winchell, Bryan's algebra teacher before he transferred out of her class. She says he can't be making such good grades on his own."

Keri's shoulders squared. "Then why hasn't she reported it to the principal?"

"She can't prove it. Neither can I. But I know in my gut it's true." He looked deeply into her eyes, trying to get through to her. "Bryan's only a junior, Keri. It's not too late for him to turn things around, maybe take summer classes so he can get a good score on the SAT."

She closed her eyes, shutting out the plea in his. When she opened them again, he could tell she'd rejected his argument. "I appreciate your concern, but I've known Bryan a lot longer than you. This isn't something he'd do."

It struck him from her formal tone that she didn't sound as though she was speaking to a man whose bed she just shared.

"He's a teenager," Grady protested. "Teenagers do lots of things they aren't supposed to."

"Not this," she said firmly. If anything, his argument seemed to accomplish the opposite of what he'd intended. She clutched at his arm. "Just tell me you're not planning to suspend him again."

He sighed. "I wouldn't suspend him without proof."

"Good." Her fingers relaxed their grip and the tension in her face eased. "Then can we drop it?"

"But—"

"Please, Grady," she interrupted. "The last time we talked about Bryan, we agreed to disagree."

She reached across the divide separating them and touched his cheek, effortlessly reestablishing the connection they'd shared all evening. "Let's not end tonight arguing. Especially when it's been such a wonderful night."

His resistance faded to nothing, like the smoke drifting up the chimney and dissipating into the dark night. With Keri gazing at him with her eyes soft and pleading, he couldn't refuse her anything.

"Sure," he said, but her grateful smile didn't dim his certainty that the topic of Bryan would surface again. And quite possibly wrench Grady and Keri apart.

CHAPTER TWELVE

BRYAN TAPPED HIS KNUCKLES on the dashboard of the undersize Kia that Jackie had borrowed from her parents, feeling cramped even though he'd slid the passenger seat back to adjust for his long legs.

"You gonna tell me why you had to drive?" he asked.

Jackie kept her eyes trained on the road and both hands firmly on the steering wheel as she drove the speed limit through Springhill. She was looking hot in a camel-colored suede jacket she wore with jeans and high-heeled boots, her blond hair long and loose.

"I like to drive on first dates," she said.

"Why?"

She flashed her pretty blue eyes at him. "Because you never can be sure how they'll go."

Bryan felt his jaw clench. He disliked thinking Jackie hadn't been enthusiastically looking forward to their date, but it was starting to appear that way. Especially since she'd turned him down for Saturday, prime date night, and suggested they go out on Sunday instead.

An overhead stoplight turned yellow. She could have easily made it through the intersection before the red light switched on, but she tapped the brakes and pulled the car to a stop.

"You don't think we'll have a good time?" he asked.

"We might," she said. "But not if you don't tell me what's bugging you."

"Besides you driving?"

"Besides that," she said agreeably.

He tapped his chin with his fist, surprised she'd picked up that something was wrong. He doubted any of the other girls he'd dated would notice. "I'm just having a bad day."

"You said on Friday this was the best time of your life," she pointed out.

"We won districts on Friday."

"Aren't there more play-offs this week?"

"Yeah," he said. The first- and second-round regional games were Tuesday and Wednesday with the semis and the championship scheduled for next weekend. If Springhill got to the championship game, the Cougars would qualify for the state tourney.

"So what's the problem?" she prodded.

He might as well tell her. "Coach Hard-Ass is making trouble for me again."

"You mean Coach Quinlan?" she asked, a hint of reproach in her voice. "Making trouble how?"

"Besides hitting on Keri?" he asked sarcastically. That was plenty bad enough. "He told her one of my teachers was changing my grades."

"Señor Myers?" she asked instantly.

"Not Señor Myers." He couldn't keep the annoyance out of his voice. "Mr. Patterson, my algebra teacher."

Her gaze seemed to pierce a hole the size of a basketball through him. "Is he?"

He threw up a hand. "Why would you even ask me that?"

"I'm in your Spanish class," she said. "I know Señor Myers treats you differently from everyone else."

The light turned green and she pressed her foot on the gas pedal. He gritted his teeth, unable to bring up any of the subjects he'd meant to talk about. Like the places she'd lived as a military brat and whether she'd let him photograph her. He thought sharing his frustration with Jackie would make him feel better, but she obviously didn't understand what being Bryan Charleton was all about.

The only movie theater within a fifteen-mile radius of Springhill was a duplex on the town's main street that was crowded only on Friday and Saturday nights. Jackie found a parking space a half block away, then walked with him up the sidewalk toward the theater. The winter weather was cooperating for once, rendering it cool instead of downright arctic.

"I can pay for my own ticket," Jackie announced, an offer he might have appreciated if it didn't seem as if she was distancing herself from him.

He waved a hand. "No need for that. We don't have to pay."

She stopped walking and turned sharply toward him. "Why not?"

He shrugged. "Because I always get in free."

"But why?"

A colorful poster for an upcoming comedy featuring Will Ferrell decorated the brick wall behind her. The way things were going, Bryan thought, he could use a laugh.

"Because of basketball, I guess."

Disapproval was stamped all over her face. "You don't

think it's wrong to get into a movie free just because you're good at basketball?"

He'd never thought about it before. "Hey, if people want to give me free stuff, I'd be crazy to say no."

"How about teachers who want to give you better grades?" she asked. "That apply to them, too?"

"Yeah, it does." He raised his voice to match the pitch of hers. "I don't know why you're making such a big deal of it."

"Because it *is* a big deal."

"Only because you don't know what you're talking about."

She visibly recoiled, and Bryan rubbed the back of his neck, feeling frustration slide through him. Why had he said that? He liked Jackie. *Really* liked her.

"That didn't come out right," he began.

A car pulled up, and a shaggy-haired kid named Phil from Bryan's history class stuck his head out the window. "Yo, Bryan. Want to come with us to Patty Franconia's?"

Bryan hardly knew Patty Franconia, but hanging out in a group was a better option than sitting in a darkened theater with a girl who disapproved of him. Jackie would be able to see how much other people liked and admired him.

"Let's go," he said to Jackie.

"You asked me to a movie."

He let out a frustrated breath. "So what? I hear the movie's not very good, anyway."

"If you didn't want to see the movie," Jackie said tightly, "you should have said so in the first place."

He angled his body between Jackie and the car. If Phil and his friends hadn't been present, he would have confided he'd sit through a Winnie the Pooh movie just to spend time with her. But he had a reputation to uphold. "I changed my mind."

"Who are those boys in the car? And who is Patty Franconia?"

"Would you stop it with the third degree," he snapped. "I get enough of that at home."

"You coming, Bryan?" Phil yelled. "Or aren't you allowed?"

"I told my parents I'd be at a movie, and that's where I'm going." Jackie turned and headed for the box office window.

Bryan's inclination was to hurry after her and apologize for being a jerk, but the boys in the car would spread it all over school that a girl ordered Bryan Charleton around.

He sauntered toward the car. "Can I get a lift?"

One of the doors opened. He took his time, not getting into the backseat until he saw that Jackie was safely inside the movie theater.

Dean Gamble, a skinny boy with stringy dark hair who spent a lot of time in detention, occupied the other half of the backseat. Dean slapped palms with Bryan while Phil put the car in Drive and pulled away. "Wait till everyone sees who we're bringing to the party," Dean said.

Party? Nobody had said anything about a party. Bryan took his cell phone out of his pocket, intending to call Hubie to pick him up. Phil turned the music on the car radio way up, and Bryan figured Hubie wouldn't be able to hear him until they reached Patty's house. He repocketed the phone.

"You're gonna have one hell of a good time, man," Phil called over his shoulder, driving about twenty miles per hour faster than the speed limit. Bryan tried to act cool but already knew getting into the car had been a mistake.

"NO DEAL!" ROSE YELLED at the contestant on the television game show. "Your case might have the million dollars!"

Keri exchanged an amused look with Grady, which Rose missed. She was too caught up with the decision facing the woman, an excitable type who kept jumping up and down. Keri would leap into the air, too, if somebody had offered her three hundred thousand dollars.

"She should take the money," Grady said. "She probably has the penny."

"No way should she settle for three hundred grand when she could have a million." Rose ignored the fact, as did most of the contestants, that the odds of winning the big money were low. The television station cut to a commercial break, and Rose groaned loudly before addressing Keri. "What do you think she should do, Keri?"

"Oh, no." Keri was comfortably ensconced between Rose and Grady on the large overstuffed sofa in the small family room, his arm draped over a back cushion, his fingers playing with the hair at Keri's nape. Delicious shivers ran down the length of her body. "I'm not taking sides."

"That's what Rachel said when she, Julie and I were watching this." Rose had been spending increasing amounts of time with the two teen girls, both of whom had run cross-country in the fall. All three of them planned to try out for the track team come spring. "But it doesn't matter what Keri would do. I'm right, and Coach Q's wrong."

Rose playfully stuck out her tongue at Grady.

"Oh, yeah?" he countered. "We'll see how wrong I am when Miss Bunny Hop opens the vault."

"The case, not the vault." Rose reached across Keri and playfully smacked Grady on the shoulder with a sofa cushion.

Keri laughed, enjoying the lighthearted interaction between them. She'd invited Grady over for a postworkout spaghetti dinner when she picked up Rose at the health club. Dinner couldn't have gone better. The conversation flowed and all three of them pitched in to clean up before Rose suggested turning on the game show.

With his stocking feet on the wooden coffee table and stubble on his lower face, Grady looked like he belonged not only in her house but in her life. He belonged in her bed, too. And she'd get him there just as soon as she could. But not when the kids were home.

She heard a car pull up outside. Wondering if it was Bryan, Keri rose from the sofa. A pretty blonde named Jackie had picked him up a few hours ago for a late-afternoon showing of a movie, but Bryan said they'd probably go to dinner afterward.

She hoped they had. She didn't want to handle the chill of Bryan's disapproval when he saw they had company.

Keri crossed to a front window and pulled a blind aside to give her a view of the street. The snow that covered their front yard and clung to the tree branches brightened the night, enabling Keri to clearly see that the car parked at the curb was a police cruiser.

Both front doors opened at once, with Bryan emerging from the passenger side. She recognized the driver as Tom Minelli, a middle-aged policeman with more hair on his face than on top of his head. Tom, his wife and two elementary-school children belonged to their church.

The theme music that signaled the game show was back from commercial break rang out from the TV. Keri glanced at Rose and Grady, confirming their attention was once again captured by the program. She left the family room to open the front door.

Bryan approached the house in front of Officer Minelli, his manner nonchalant, as though the police drove him home every day. At first glance she thought he looked ashen, the way he had when those boys tried to pick a fight beside the concession stand. But his paleness could have been due to the porch light washing out his complexion.

"What's going on?" Keri asked.

"It's nothing," he muttered, moving past her into the house.

"I told you she shouldn't take the deal!" Rose's cry of delight drifted to where they were standing. Bryan stuck his head in the entrance to the family room, his eyes growing colder than the February night when he turned back to Keri. "What's Coach doing here?"

Keri didn't appreciate his tone or his attitude. "You're not in a position to ask questions before I get answers."

Bryan pivoted, heading for the staircase and calling, "I'll be in my room."

He stomped up the steps. Keri was about to order him back downstairs when Officer Minelli reached the doorstep. She gathered her composure. "Please come in, Officer Minelli."

"Call me Tom," he said heartily, as though he hadn't witnessed Keri's unpleasant exchange with Bryan.

Grady emerged from the family room as Keri was shutting the front door, a questioning expression on his face. Tom Minelli stuck out his right hand and introduced himself. "Coach Quinlan, isn't it? You've got one hell of a basketball team."

"Thanks," Grady said.

Keri heard dresser drawers opening and banging shut in Bryan's room while the two men shook hands. She felt her face heat. "I don't know what's come over Bryan. He usually doesn't act like this."

"I expect he's shaken up after what happened," Tom Minelli said.

"What did happen?" Keri asked.

The policeman immediately looked at Grady, making it easy for Keri to read what was on his mind.

"It's okay. Anything you have to say, you can say in front of Grady." Keri edged closer to Grady, grateful for his silent support when he put a hand on her shoulder.

Tom Minelli nodded briefly. "Bryan was at the wrong place at the wrong time. A party at the house of a girl named Patty Franconia. You know her?"

Keri shook her head.

"Somebody called the cops because the music was too loud. The parents weren't home and some kids were drinking. We took a couple of them into the station."

Keri's hand flew to her throat. She felt Grady's hand tighten on her shoulder. "Was Bryan drinking?"

"He said no." The policeman's tone was matter-of-fact. "My understanding is this wasn't his usual crowd and he was waiting on a friend to pick him up. So I put him in my car and drove him home." The policeman winked at Grady. "No need getting him in trouble before regionals."

"Thank you, Tom," Keri said. "I appreciate it, and I'm sure Bryan does, too."

"Anytime." He announced he needed to be going and left.

Rose appeared seconds after Keri closed the door on the policeman, her young face screwed up with concern. "Everything all right?"

"Everything's fine. The policeman was just doing us a favor." Keri tried to smile at Rose. "Why don't you say goodbye to Grady and go upstairs and take a shower?"

Rose seemed as though she wanted to ask more questions, but then nodded slowly. "Okay. Bye, Coach Q."

"Bye, Zoom Zoom," he said, earning himself a smile.

Keri watched Rose's progress, waiting until her daughter was no longer visible before allowing her shoulders to slump. When the blonde had picked up Bryan earlier, Keri never expected him to arrive home in a police car.

"Why would Bryan go to a party with regionals coming up?" She voiced the question uppermost in her mind. She was well aware, as was Bryan, that the school had a no-tolerance policy when alcohol and drugs were involved.

Grady took her hand, leading her away from the staircase into the family room, proving he was thinking more clearly than she was. She didn't want either of her children to overhear their conversation.

She was too upset to sit down. Grady seemed to understand that, turning her around so his strong fingers could massage the rigid muscles in her shoulders. "Bryan wasn't thinking."

He couldn't have been. Keri sometimes thanked God basketball meant so much to Bryan, believing the strict rules the school applied to its athletes assured he'd steer clear of trouble.

"At least he dodged a bullet," Keri said, thinking aloud. "It would have been so much worse if you had to suspend him."

His fingers stilled, and she could feel tension emanating not from her but from him. "I do have to suspend him."

She spun to face Grady, and his hands dropped from her shoulders. She knew she'd heard him correctly but couldn't make sense of his words. "What? You heard Tom Minelli. Bryan wasn't even drinking."

"Bryan *said* he wasn't drinking." Grady's face, with the uncompromising set of his lips, looked like that of a stranger. "Doesn't matter either way. Bryan was at a party with alcohol. School policy's clear on what I have to do."

"You could make an exception!" Keri said.

"Bryan won't learn anything if I don't suspend him."

"You're suspending me?" Bryan's incredulous voice rang out. The boy stood steps inside the family room, those big, dark eyes he inherited from Maddy wide and disbelieving. "You can't do that!"

KERI TOOK A STEP closer to Bryan. And farther away from Grady.

When they'd discussed Bryan in front of the fireplace last night, Grady suspected their polar views on the boy might pull them apart. He'd never expected it to happen so soon.

"I can," Grady said calmly, "and I will."

Bryan's face crumbled at the implications of a suspension, and Grady ached for him. At times Keri seemed desperate to convince Grady that Bryan was a good kid, but Grady already knew that. He wouldn't be as hard on Bryan if he didn't.

"But…but…" Bryan seemed to be desperately searching for an argument that would change Grady's mind. "But you won't win without me!"

"Then we won't win," Grady said.

"This is so unfair," Bryan lashed out, reminding Grady of a trapped, wounded animal. "You wouldn't know about the party if you hadn't been here."

"I am here," Grady said. "And I'm not changing my mind."

"Then you're a son of a—"

"Bryan! I won't allow you to speak to a guest in our house that way," Keri interrupted, her voice more harsh than Grady had ever heard it. "Go to your room."

"But I—"

"You heard me," Keri said sternly. "Go to your room."

Bryan appeared about to protest, but then dashed up the stairs, as he'd done after the cop delivered him to the door.

Grady waited until Bryan was gone. "Thanks."

"If you're thanking me because you think I agree with you, stop right there," she said in a quiet voice no less furious than it had been before Bryan left the room. "Didn't you see his face? Couldn't you tell how upset he is?"

"Yes," Grady said.

"Then why suspend him? What will that teach him? That his coach is as much of a hard-ass as he already thinks he is?"

Keri hadn't touched him, but it felt to Grady as though each one of her words had left a mark.

"Is that what you think of me, too?" Grady asked in a low voice.

"I think you're a hypocrite. Holding Bryan to impossible standards while…" Her voice trailed off, but he already knew what she was about to say.

"While what?" he challenged, his voice hard, inflexible.

"While behaving dishonorably yourself," she retorted, confirming his suspicion. "Don't you see what you're doing? You're punishing Bryan for making a mistake not nearly as bad as yours. And why? To prove you can run a clean program?"

After all the time they'd spent together, she still believed him to be a liar and a cheat. Grady's chest tightened so it felt as if a vise was squeezing his heart. But he couldn't take only himself into account, not with a teenage boy's future at stake.

"No matter what you think of me, you need to open your eyes to what's going on with Bryan," he said flatly.

"Bryan's a great kid," she said stubbornly. Again.

"Bryan's playing you. Teachers change his grades, classmates do his work, businessmen give him free stuff." He gestured to the foyer, where Tom Minelli had winked at him. "Hell, even the police treat him differently."

"People like Bryan," she said, as though she hadn't paid attention to a word he said.

"They like that he's a good basketball player."

Her chin adopted a defiant angle. "Bryan has a lot more going for him than basketball."

"Then don't make the mistake of letting him put basketball above everything else in his life."

Keri's chest heaved. "I'll tell you what my mistake was. It was getting involved with you."

Grady's mistake was falling for a woman who wouldn't believe in him. At that realization, he could barely speak over the painful lump in his throat.

"Then this is it?" he asked, taking a step closer to her and pressing the issue. "We're through?"

Tears glistened in her eyes, confirming for him that she wasn't unaffected by the moment. In a soft voice, she said, "We never should have begun."

He nearly asked whether that was because they disagreed over Bryan or because she hadn't changed her opinion of Grady, but couldn't bear to hear the answer.

Without another word, he walked out of her house. And her life.

CHAPTER THIRTEEN

THE STRONG SCENT OF COFFEE seemed to saturate the very
air of the small, homey shop, causing Grady to feel as
though he'd gulped some caffeine even before he approached the counter.

The instant pick-me-up was one of the reasons he made
a habit of stopping at Café Coffee on weekday mornings
before school started. The clerk—correction, the barista—
who usually waited on him was another draw. A mother
of three named Frannie, she liked to talk. Sports, current
events, politics. She'd hit on all of those topics in the
months Grady had been stopping by.

"Hey, Frannie," he said when he reached the front of
the short line.

The smile she usually greeted him with was absent, and
she didn't quite meet his eyes. "What'll it be?"

He always ordered the same thing, and it wasn't
espresso, latte or cappuccino. "A regular coffee. Black."

Instead of teasing him about his lack of imagination or
chattering away about whatever came to mind, Frannie
nodded curtly and went to fill his order. Yesterday she'd
been her usual vivacious self, cheerfully complaining
about the solution her youngest child had come up with

to get their new puppy to stop crying through the night. He snuck the dog into his bed.

Frannie set his cup of coffee on the gleaming wood of the counter, efficiently ringing up the sale even before he removed his wallet from his back pocket.

"Everything all right, Frannie?" he asked.

She didn't meet his eyes. "Everything's fine."

He withdrew a five dollar bill from his wallet and handed it to her. "The new puppy still bunking with Joey?"

"No," she said, reaching into the slots of the cash register to make change and handing it over.

Before he could tell her to have a good day, like he always did, she gazed past him to the next customer and asked, "Can I help you?"

"Not just yet," Mary Lynn Marco said, her red coat matching the spots on her cheeks and her curly blond hair looking wilder than usual.

Grady had run into Mary Lynn at Café Coffee on a few other occasions, but she was usually in a great rush to get to her job as a receptionist for a local construction company. Her refusal to grab a cup of coffee and go wasn't the only thing off kilter about Mary Lynn.

Her ever-present smile was missing.

"Hey, Mary Lynn," Grady said.

"I'm glad I caught you." Mary Lynn's gaze swept the interior of the shop, causing Grady to note that Frannie and the customers occupying the nearest tables regarded them with interest. "Will you sit with me for a while?"

He knew without checking his watch he wasn't in danger of being late, but Mary Lynn might be. "You sure you have time?"

"Work can wait. This can't," she said mysteriously before claiming the table farthest from the other customers. Even that was uncharacteristic. The extroverted Mary Lynn liked being around people.

Once they were seated, he asked the obvious question. "Things okay with Tony?"

A shadow seemed to chase across her face.

"Everything's about the same. I can't get pregnant. He's never home. Blah, blah, blah." She waved a hand. "But I'm not here to talk about Tony. Did you read this morning's *Gazette*?"

"Not yet."

"The paper's reporting you suspended Bryan Charleton."

Grady nodded. He'd informed his players after last night's practice that Bryan wouldn't be playing in the first round of regionals. "I expected that."

"There's more, Grady." Her expression appeared as pained as when she'd confided in him about her fractured marriage. "A second story tells what happened at Carolina State."

When his back teeth ground against one another, it occurred to him that he'd clenched his jaw. He deliberately relaxed his facial muscles, striving not to show the news bothered him. It shouldn't. He'd always known it was inevitable that news of the scandal would get out.

"It's not good, Grady," Mary Lynn said in a hushed voice. "It makes it sound like you were totally in the wrong. I told Tony that was because the reporter didn't talk to you. Couldn't be reached for comment, is what he wrote."

Grady had stopped for a bite to eat after practice last

night and arrived home after nine. He couldn't remember if he'd checked his answering machine, but didn't think so.

"We didn't want you to get blindsided by this," she said. Too late, Grady thought. "Tony tried calling to warn you but couldn't reach you. I knew you stopped by here sometimes so I said I'd try to catch you."

"I appreciate it," Grady said, futilely wishing the story had broke after regionals. Hell, who was he kidding? He wished the news hadn't surfaced at all.

"It just makes me so mad the reporter didn't get your side of the story," Mary Lynn said.

Grady told his side to the Carolina State administration and got fired, anyway. He tried to stuff himself back into his invisible suit of armor, but it didn't fit. Things had been going so well at Springhill, he no longer thought he needed to protect himself against barbs and incriminations.

He averted his gaze from Mary Lynn while he tried to rebuild his defenses. He noticed the stack of newspapers beside the cash register before his eyes locked with Frannie's. She quickly looked away.

"If only you hadn't suspended Bryan," Mary Lynn lamented.

"Bryan needed to be suspended." Grady gruffly stated his increasingly unpopular position. Word had spread about Bryan calling a friend to pick him up from the party. The things Bryan had done that reflected badly on him remained largely unknown.

"Yeah, but the timing stinks." Mary Lynn's brow crinkled. "Do you think Bryan leaked the story?"

"Could be," Grady said. Bryan had poured maximum

effort into every drill and line sprint at last night's practice, possibly believing he could get Grady to revoke the suspension through sheer effort. He'd stormed out of the gym when Grady restated his penalty. "That's assuming Bryan knew I coached at Carolina State."

"Who besides Tony and me did know?" Mary Lynn asked.

Keri, Grady thought.

Mary Lynn seemed to read his mind. "Tony said you and Keri are dating."

"We *were* dating." His use of the past tense produced a physical ache. He often lay awake dreaming up basketball plays, but the past two nights he'd replayed the ugly scene with Keri. He couldn't dredge up any anger, only sadness. "We're not dating anymore."

Mary Lynn brought both hands to her cheeks. "Oh, that's not good. You know she works for the *Gazette*, right? What am I saying? Of course you know."

"What are you implying?" Grady asked, but he already understood.

"Isn't it obvious?" Mary Lynn's blue eyes turned wide and sympathetic. "Keri must be the source."

"DID YOU READ THE newspaper yet?"

Jill McMann, fashionably dressed in an icy-green turtleneck and black crochet skirt, fired the question at Keri before Keri settled into her workstation.

"You must be joking. I don't have time to read the paper until I get to work." Keri maneuvered out of her quilted jacket and hung it on the coat rack between their cubicles. "And good morning to you, too."

"You won't think it's a good morning after you read the sports section."

Jill had made sure Keri wouldn't miss it. The newspaper lay across Keri's keyboard, the stories above the fold visible. There were two of them, positioned around a photo of Grady and topped with the main heading, *Courting Trouble.*

Springhill Coach Suspends Star read the first headline. But the second was the one that made Keri's stomach lurch. *Quinlan Was Key Figure in Recruiting Scandal.*

Keri quickly read the lead.

Springhill High coach Grady Quinlan was fired from the Carolina State basketball coaching staff two seasons ago for recruiting violations that nearly toppled the program.

The rest of the article provided no new information, but the tale seemed more inconceivable. Keri found it increasingly difficult to rationalize what she knew about Grady with what he'd done.

She quickly read through the rest of the story, searching for a quote from Grady, hoping his response to the charges would help her come to grips with the two contradictory views of him. Instead she read the line, *Quinlan could not be reached for comment.*

"Pretty volatile stuff." Jill leaned against the side of Keri's cubicle, her legs crossed at the ankles. "Did you know about Carolina State?"

"I knew," Keri said.

Jill's teeth showed when she winced. "That could be sticky. You know what Grady'll think, right?"

Keri put herself in Grady's position. She heard herself

call him a hypocrite and angrily criticize him for suspending Bryan.

"Oh, no." She covered her mouth before letting her fingers drop. "He'll think I leaked the story."

"You did just break up with him," Jill pointed out.

Keri picked up the phone beside her computer, punched in the numbers of Grady's cell and listened to the unanswered rings. Of course. It was the beginning of the school day. Grady would be in class.

"Grady, this is Keri," she said almost before the beep sounded, eager to get out the words. "I wanted you to know I had nothing to do with the story in today's paper."

She was on her feet before she disconnected the call, grabbing the paper to check the bylines over the stories.

"Now what?" Jill asked.

"Now Will Schneider is going to tell me how he found out about Grady and Carolina State," she said.

The advertising department and the newsroom occupied opposite ends of the same floor. As she hurried across the divide toward the sports department, Keri acknowledged the unlikelihood of finding a reporter who'd worked late the night before at his desk. But there was Will Schneider, head bent over his keyboard, industriously tapping away.

Although advertising and editorial employees were usually kept separate, Keri was acquainted with Will because of their shared interest in Springhill basketball. She marched straight up to his desk. "Can I talk to you for a minute?"

He glanced up at her while his fingers continued to fly over the keyboard. A small man with a bounce to his step and an intense air, he always seemed to be in a hurry. Stubble covered his lower face and his clothes looked a tad rumpled, as though he'd tumbled out of bed and come directly to work. "Talk fast. I've got an appointment soon."

"Who told you about Grady Quinlan and Carolina State?"

He stopped typing and awarded her his full attention. "You know I can't reveal my sources."

"The information is a matter of public record," Keri argued. "I just want to know how you found out about it."

He crossed his arms over his chest and jutted out his chin. "And I'm not telling you."

She mentally reviewed a list of his possible reasons for remaining quiet and settled on one. "Was it one of the Springhill players?"

He said nothing, but her mind raced. The Cougar with the biggest grudge against Grady lived in her house. "It was Bryan, wasn't it?"

Will pressed his lips together before answering, symbolically underscoring that she was wasting her time. "I'm not saying one way or the other."

She left him, the suspicion causing her to feel even worse. She'd like to believe Bryan hadn't retaliated against Grady for suspending him, but her twisting gut told her that might not be the case.

AFTER SEVERAL UNSUCCESSFUL calls to Grady during the day, she phoned the school secretary and discovered he was teaching a PE class last period. She rejected her initial idea to intercept him at the gym, deciding after she got a visitor's pass to wait for him outside his office.

En route to the wing of the school where the athletic offices were located, she spotted a Springhill cheerleader in uniform, as was the custom with a big game on the horizon. Upon closer inspection, she saw that it was Becky Harding.

The petite, dark-haired cheerleader was alone, what looked to be a hall pass clutched in her hand.

"Becky," Keri called. "Remember me?"

Becky turned warily, nodded slowly, her bangs rustling with the movement. *Go Cougars* was written in gold-and-black greasepaint on one of her cheeks, which also sported a tiny heart. "You're Bryan's mom."

"That's right."

Becky didn't move, but Keri had the impression her muscles were coiled, so she could instantly put distance between them. "I had nothing to do with Bryan getting suspended this time."

"I know," Keri assured her.

Becky seemed to relax, but not entirely. "Good. Because I don't need people on my case again. It was hard enough lying to Coach Quinlan once to get Bryan out of trouble."

Keri mentally reviewed the sequence of events, recalling Becky had recanted her initial claim that she'd written Bryan's paper. "You mean you lied to get Bryan *in* trouble."

"No," Becky said firmly. "I wrote the paper. And it wasn't because I had some stupid crush on Bryan, like everyone said. It was because Jeremiah asked me to."

Jeremiah Bowden, Becky's boyfriend and one of Bryan's closest friends.

Keri stared wordlessly at Becky while the pieces finally clicked together. Grady's assessment of the situation had been correct. Becky only changed her story because of pressure from classmates.

"Anything else?" Becky asked, already backing away. "Because I've got to go."

"No," Keri said slowly. "That's all."

Keri continued down the hall toward Grady's office, her thoughts spinning. Since Grady had been right about the paper, it stood to reason his other charges also had merit.

It was no longer impossible to believe that Jack Patterson was changing Bryan's grades. Or that the deal Bryan got on his used car at the Honda dealership really was too good to be true. Or even that the reason Bryan seldom asked for money was that he usually got a free ride wherever he went.

Keri reached Grady's office and leaned against the wall outside the door. She placed a hand over her forehead, hardly believing she could have been so blind. Or so stupid.

The bell rang, signaling the last class of the day had ended. Grady appeared in the distance shortly afterward, dressed in a gold Springhill basketball T-shirt and black sweatpants. His step faltered when he spotted her, but he kept coming, his expression revealing none of his feelings.

"Keri." He inclined his head slightly, the greeting no colder than Keri deserved. The realization brought her no comfort.

She straightened from the wall and gathered her resolve. "I'm sorry to show up like this, but I wasn't sure if you got my voice mails."

His eyes, usually so full of sparkle and life, seemed flat. "I haven't checked my phone."

A few teachers and students she didn't recognize, half of them dressed in school colors, passed by, glancing curiously at them. She looked longingly toward his office, hoping he'd invite her inside so they could speak privately. He didn't take the hint, his manner toward her detached.

"I owe you an apology." She swallowed, but her throat was parched. "I shouldn't have doubted that Becky Harding wrote Bryan's paper."

A flicker of surprise crossed his face, the first emotion he'd shown. "What brought this on?"

"I ran into Becky just now, and she admitted it." Keri bit down on her lower lip, forcing herself to face the ramifications of Becky's confession. "I need to talk to Jack Patterson and find out if he's changing Bryan's grades."

He nodded slowly. "Yes, you do. For Bryan's sake."

He moved past her toward his office, silently dismissing her. She put a hand on his arm to detain him, feeling the familiar warmth of his skin and the unfamiliar tension in his muscles. He stopped but didn't look at her. She dropped her hand.

"There's more," she said. "I need you to know I had nothing to do with that story in today's paper."

His eyes flicked to her face. "I know that."

Confusion tempered the relief that coursed through her. How could Grady know she hadn't been responsible? "Did Will Schneider tell you that?"

"No."

"Then I don't understand. Why are you sure I didn't leak the story?"

"Because I know what kind of person you are, Keri. You wouldn't do something like that." He didn't come out and say she should have given him the same benefit of the doubt, but he didn't have to. He shuffled his feet. "Is that it? Because I have a game to get ready for."

"That's it," Keri said softly before he walked into his office and the door shut with a decisive click.

TONY MARCO MIGHT NOT HAVE spotted Keri if he hadn't been headed to Grady's office to tell his cousin about the repercussions of this morning's newspaper stories.

Fuzz Cartwright, the former head basketball coach, had reamed out Tony for what Fuzz referred to as a "hiring mistake." The president of the athletic boosters club advocated firing Grady and assigning the junior-varsity coach to handle the regional games. Countless others advised Tony to order Grady to lift Bryan Charleton's suspension.

No question Tony and Grady had a hell of a lot to talk about, including Tony's intention to do none of those things.

So it made no sense that Tony was currently driving through Springhill about three car lengths behind Keri's Volvo.

He tried catching up after he saw her leave Grady's office, but she walked quickly out of the building and to her car in the visitor's lot. Next thing Tony knew, he was inside his own car and pursuing her.

He couldn't pinpoint a reason. Keri had been straightforward about her lack of interest in resuming their relationship. The relief that had overtaken him at her rejection was more complicated.

It defied logic, especially because he and Mary Lynn weren't getting along. They'd gone another round this morning on a variation of the subject consuming their lives.

"I don't understand why you won't get tested," Mary Lynn had complained.

"Why should I? We already know you have ovulation problems."

"But the doctor won't put me on fertility drugs until we rule out other factors. Even with my problem, he said it would be hard, but not impossible, for me to get pregnant."

He'd rubbed his brow, the strain of the past six months overwhelming him. "This whole situation is impossible."

"I'll tell you what's impossible," Mary Lynn had shot back. "It's impossible for me to get pregnant when we've stopped having sex."

He'd barely kept from groaning. "Don't tell me your body temperature chart says it's time for us to get it on."

She'd crossed her arms over her chest and lifted her chin. "As a matter of fact, it does."

"What do you expect from me, Mary Lynn? To sweep the cornflakes off the kitchen table and do you right here, right now?"

Her lower lip had trembled, making him feel like a jerk. "You didn't used to need an excuse to make love to me."

He couldn't remember the details of the rest of their argument, but he could still hear the door banging shut behind him when he'd left the house.

Keri's Volvo signaled a right turn into the *Springhill Gazette* parking lot and Tony realized with a start they'd arrived at the newspaper office. He spied an empty spot along the curb in front of the building and swung his car into the space. He'd barely shut off the engine when he heard a tapping on his car window.

Keri stood at the curb glaring down at him, so close to the car he had to roll down the window instead of opening the door.

"Keri." He flashed her a huge smile she didn't return.

"What are you doing here, Tony?" she asked in what was beginning to sound like a familiar refrain. She'd said the same thing when he came to her house Sunday.

He hadn't thought far enough ahead to formulate a legitimate excuse so he invented one on the spot. "Placing a classified ad."

"In person?" she asked skeptically, clueing him that most classified advertising was done over the phone. "For what?"

Her penetrating stare froze his vocal chords. "You got me," he said sheepishly. "I'm not here to place a classified."

"You followed me, didn't you?" she asked, steel in her voice. "Don't bother to deny it. I saw you in the high school parking lot."

"Okay. I followed you," he admitted.

"This has to stop, Tony," she said. The bright sun warmed the February afternoon, casting little doubt that the color staining her cheeks was caused by temper. "Not only because of me, but because of Mary Lynn. Why did you marry her if you were going to run around on her?"

"I'm not—" he began.

She didn't give him the chance to tell her he'd never been unfaithful to his wife.

"It's not fair to Mary Lynn," she continued. "Anybody who sees you together can tell how much she loves you, but if you don't love her you shouldn't have—"

"I do love her," he interrupted, much louder and more forcefully than he'd intended. And he did love Mary Lynn. He could even pinpoint when it had begun. He'd been visiting his parents shortly after the breakup with Keri and went into town to pick up a gallon of milk for his mother. Mary Lynn had emerged from the store, her arms straining from carrying too many grocery bags, but her smile was in place. The sun had been shining on her blond hair, but her glow seemed to come from within.

"If you love Mary Lynn," Keri asked in a quieter voice, "why are you hitting on me?"

Because he was a blind idiot. He started to say as much, but she spoke first.

"Because no matter what you do or say," she continued, "I am not going to have an affair with you."

"That's not what I want, either."

She placed her hands on her hips, confusion stamped on her features. He didn't blame her. He could hardly figure himself out.

"Then what exactly is it you want from me?" she asked.

He hadn't known the answer until she asked the question, but now it resounded inside him. "Forgiveness."

She cocked her head but said nothing.

The truth hit him hard, but the fact must have come over him so gradually he hadn't noticed.

"I should have supported you when you took in Rose and Bryan," he said. "I never should have made you choose between us."

How stupid he'd been to view children as a nuisance rather than a treasure. It had taken the possibility that he might never father a child to open his eyes.

"I accept your apology," she said. They were exactly the words he needed to hear. She laid a hand on his arm. "But it all worked out for the best. You and me, we're not supposed to be together."

"Because you love Grady," he said, any trace of jealousy at the thought gone.

She averted her eyes, but not before he glimpsed the sadness in them. "We're not dating anymore."

He grimaced, guilt crashing down on him for the way he'd reacted when he guessed she was seeing his cousin. "It's not because of what I said, is it? Because Grady's a great guy. He—"

"Our breakup had nothing to do with you," she interrupted. "When I said we're not supposed to be together, I meant you're supposed to be with Mary Lynn."

"Thanks," he said, knowing she was right. "But I don't know if I can fix what's wrong between us. I haven't been a good husband."

"But you are a good man," she said. "I wouldn't have spent a year with you if you weren't. I'm sure you're smart enough to figure out how to make things up to Mary Lynn."

He thought of the argument he'd had with his wife this morning. Scheduling an appointment with an infertility specialist would make his wife happy. "I've already got an idea."

"Good," Keri said. She bent down, stuck her head inside the open window and brushed his cheek with her lips.

"What was that for?" he asked after she drew back.

"Coming to your senses," she said.

He smiled at that and was still smiling when he pulled away from the curb. He considered himself to be a lucky man. Not only was he married to one terrific woman, he'd shared part of his past with another.

CHAPTER FOURTEEN

KERI PAUSED STEPS INSIDE the entrance to the high school gym and flipped open the screen of her cell phone. Her most recent text message still displayed the four words Bryan had sent earlier that day: *Don't worry. I'm fine.*

A teenage boy bumped her, apologized and kept going. She shut the phone, then took better note of her surroundings and the people trying to squeeze past her.

At ten minutes to game time, the court was surrounded on four sides by bleachers filling fast with fans. Everybody in Springhill and Newington, the two schools squaring off in the first round of the regional tournament, seemed to have made the twenty-mile trip to the neutral high school hosting the contest.

Everybody but Bryan.

Bryan's Cougar teammates were warming up on court in the spacious gym reported to be the largest in the state.

The stakes were high. The winner would survive to play another day, but the loser's season ended tonight. The most ardent Springhill fans were already standing and chanting while the Cougar cheerleaders waved their pom-poms. Yet Bryan wasn't at courtside, like a suspended player should be.

Keri had no idea of his whereabouts. He hadn't come home after school, he hadn't taken the bus to the game with his teammates, and he seemed to have turned off his cell phone after sending her that cryptic text message.

She wasn't worried but she was angry, more so at herself than at Bryan.

He should know better than to accept favors because he was good at basketball, but she should have noticed that people were giving him handouts.

"Keri!" Lori Patterson appeared at her elbow, beaming up at her. She was coatless and carrying a large soft drink and a box of popcorn. "Did you just get here?"

"Five minutes ago," Keri replied.

"We saved you a seat," Lori said, as if there was no question Keri would sit with the usual crowd. Her bleacher buddies, Keri had called them in happier days. A buzzer sounded, indicating the warm-up period was over. "Come on. We've got to hurry so we don't miss anything."

Keri cast a final glance at the entrance to the gym, fruitlessly hoping to see Bryan striding through the doors. His eleventh-hour appearance might take the edge off her displeasure, but then again it might not. Maybe nothing could.

Before they reached the bleachers on the Springhill side of the court, the national anthem began to play. Keri covered her heart with her right hand and felt it racing, not because of Bryan but because of the ramifications to Grady if Springhill lost the game.

Grady stood on court with his players, his hand over his heart like hers, appearing as calm and collected as always. He'd changed into a gold dress shirt and black slacks, looking so handsome and so dear that her heart hurt when she thought of the terrible things she'd said to him. A hypocrite, she'd called him.

"Come on," Lori said when the last strains of "The Star-Spangled Banner" faded. As the starting lineups were being announced, Lori led Keri up the bleacher steps to seats directly behind the Springhill bench. Frankie Polkowski's parents, Lori's ex-husband, Jack, and their little girl were already there. So was Carolyn Brown, Hubie's mom. Carolyn patted the seat next to her. "Sit next to me, Keri."

Keri was tempted to refuse so she could park herself next to Jack Patterson and tell him in strong language that she disapproved of him inflating Bryan's grades. But that meeting would have to wait until Monday, when she planned to make a long-overdue trip to the school. Resigned, Keri sat next to Carolyn.

Conversation proved impossible, which suited Keri fine. A few hundred Springhill students, wearing "Cougar Power" T-shirts and cheering loudly enough to bust a decibel counter, had positioned themselves a section over from the parents.

Newington, Springhill's opponent, was a surprise contender that got by on hustle and superior team defense, two of the things Grady also stressed. The two teams, looking like carbon copies, traded baskets in a low-scoring first half. True to his coaching style, Grady used all his players, although the better players got more minutes.

He was quick to pat a player on the back and give a word of encouragement when they came off the floor. With the game tied at the half, he looked like the calmest person in the gym.

"This is so exciting I can hardly stand it." Lori dramatically placed the back of her right hand over her forehead as though she might faint.

Carolyn leaned over to remark, "Yeah, but it wouldn't be close if we had a different coach."

Keri's temper bubbled, and she struggled to keep it on simmer as the Newington High step team was introduced. "I think Grady's doing a good job."

"Oh, my gosh. I didn't just hear that, did I?" Carolyn Brown had a confrontational way of speaking that never failed to put Keri on edge. "Why would you stick up for him?"

A dozen or so male and female students, clad entirely in black, took the court.

"Because it's true," Keri said. "He is doing a good job."

Carolyn harrumphed, talking over the rhythmic clapping and energetic stomping of dozens of feet. "Maybe in this game, but not this season."

"He got the team this far, didn't he?"

"*Bryan* got the team this far, and then what does Quinlan do?" Carolyn answered her own question. "He suspends him."

"Grady suspended Bryan for being at a party where there was alcohol."

"Bryan ended up at that party by mistake!" Carolyn retorted. "Hubie was on his way to pick him up."

It was the same case Keri had presented when Grady informed her he was suspending Bryan. Now that Keri knew about the special favors Bryan received, the argument didn't sound as rational. "Grady's looking out for Bryan's best interests."

"What's with you, Keri?" Carolyn's lip curled and disgust coated her syllables. "Quinlan's a cheat and a liar."

"He is not," Keri rejoined angrily.

On court the members of the step team, performing without music, picked up its pace, the rapid stamps of their feet sounding almost angry.

Carolyn recoiled but didn't stop talking. "Then you must not read the newspaper."

"I read the stories," Keri said. "And I don't care what the people at Carolina State say. Grady didn't do those things."

"Then who did?" Carolyn challenged.

"Not Grady," Keri said with absolute conviction. She stood up. "Now, if you'll excuse me. I'm going to find another seat."

Without another word, she squeezed past Lori, the Polkowskis and Jack Patterson. Judging by their open mouths, they'd heard the entire conversation. Good, Keri thought as she tramped down the bleacher stairs in concert with the step team.

She located a seat only a few rows behind the Springhill bench, settling into it as the step team finished its performance. Soon afterward, the Cougar players sprinted onto the court from the direction of the locker room, trailed by Grady and Sid Humphries, the JV coach still acting as his assistant.

Grady turned his dark head toward the stands and swept the crowd with his gaze. His eyes locked on hers, as though he'd found what he was searching for.

Her breathing quickened and her heartbeat sped up as she realized that every word she'd spoken to the annoying Carolyn Brown was true. Grady Quinlan was an honorable and decent man, something she must have known on a visceral level almost from the moment they met.

She nodded, hoping the action would silently convey her support. He nodded back, his expression unfathomable. When he broke eye contact, she felt an overpowering sense of loss.

Because not only was Grady Quinlan everything a man should be, she was in love with him.

BRYAN DROPPED THE KEY to the front door on the concrete of the sidewalk in front of his house, picked it up and blew warm breath over his fingers.

He'd spent the first part of the afternoon taking photographs of random landscapes and the second shooting hoops by himself at an outdoor court that only days ago had been covered by snow. His hands still hadn't thawed, but he supposed he should be grateful he could walk. He'd tweaked an ankle when he stepped on a large stone he hadn't noticed.

Then again it was pretty damn hard to give thanks for being in playing shape when Coach Hard-Ass wouldn't let him play.

He let himself into the house, then groaned aloud when he heard noises coming from upstairs. He should have checked the garage for Keri's car. He'd waited until now to come home because he thought she'd be at the game.

"Who's there?" somebody called. Rose, not Keri. His shoulders slumped in relief.

"Bryan," he answered.

His sister ran easily down the stairs. "Everybody keeps calling here looking for you," she said.

"Everybody who?"

"Keri. Hubie. And some girl who didn't leave her name. She called two or three times."

Bryan spread his arms. "Well, here I am."

"But aren't you supposed to be at the game?"

He didn't feel like answering her, but did, anyway. "Coach Hard-Ass suspended me, remember?"

"Don't call him that," Rose said testily as though he'd insulted *her.*

"Why not? He's a jerk."

"Coach Q is wonderful," she retorted. "You're the jerk."

Bryan felt as though Rose had slapped him. She'd never said anything like that to him before.

"I don't care if you are suspended," Rose continued in the same unsympathetic tone. "You're supposed to be with your team."

His conscience panged, but he covered it up with a scoff. "You're not at the game."

A car horn sounded, and Rose grabbed her coat from the hall closet. "That's because tonight is Rachel's cosmic bowling birthday party. Her mom's picking me up."

She walked out the door into the night without another word, leaving it standing wide open. *Great,* Bryan thought sarcastically. *My little sister's gone over to the dark side.*

He was about to let the front door swing shut when he saw Jackie Fitzgibbons approaching the house. In jeans and a darker blue jeans jacket, her blond hair hanging long and loose, she looked beautiful.

She stopped dead when she saw him, speaking first. "I'm only here because Hubie text messaged. Guess you didn't tell him I wasn't speaking to you."

Bryan was wise enough not to point out the contrary was true at the moment. "What does Hubie want?"

"He wants you to get your butt to the game," she said, obviously repeating Hubie's order verbatim. She spun, golden hair flying, and retreated toward where her car was parked at the curb.

"Wait," Bryan called, running down the sidewalk and catching up to her in the front yard.

She turned, her expression stoic. "What?"

He unclenched his jaw with difficulty and drew a deep breath. "I was a jerk the other night," he said, using the same term Rose had used.

"Yeah, you were," she readily agreed before turning and walking to her car.

As apologies went, he knew his had been lacking. "I'm sorry, okay?" he called after her.

Her back squared. She stopped moving but didn't turn around. "Sorry's not good enough."

He circled around to face her, desperate to get her to see things his way. "Look. I really like you. I want us to keep hanging out, okay?"

"You're not a bad guy," Jackie said, "but I can't be around someone like you."

Someone like him? He was Bryan Charleton. "I don't understand."

"Then let me ask you something. Why did you get in the car with those guys, anyway?"

He shrugged. "I don't know. I guess I didn't want them to think I was…uncool."

"Getting suspended was uncool."

"Coach shouldn't have suspended me," Bryan said, his

bitterness spilling over into his words. "I wasn't even drinking."

"Yeah, I forgot. You're like a Boy Scout."

"What's that supposed to mean?"

She shook her head. "I'm not blind, Bryan. I go to Springhill, too. I can see what's going on. You think I don't know Anna Baranski writes your English papers?"

"She does n—"

"She showed me one," she interrupted. "And how come you get free food in the cafeteria?"

"So what if I do?"

"It's wrong, Bryan, and you can't even see it. I mean, look at you. You're not even at the game tonight."

"I told you why," he said with tight lips. "I didn't deserve to be suspended."

"Maybe not for being at the party, but there are a bunch of other reasons your coach could have suspended you."

"But—"

She put up a hand. "Just stop, Bryan. I don't want to hear it."

This time she didn't stop walking until she reached her car. After she drove away, he stood out in the cold for a long time thinking about what she'd said.

He knew he'd lost her, but he could gain something back that was equally as important.

His self-respect.

KERI PACED FROM ONE END of her house to the other, too jazzed to sit down. Springhill's season had ended about an hour ago, with the team putting up a gallant fight but falling short of moving on to the next round by a basket.

She'd filed out of the gym with the unhappy faithful, over-hearing more than one angry fan blaming the loss on Grady.

"Bryan Charleton wasn't even in the gym," the most vocal of the disappointed fans had said. "That tells you what he thinks of the coach."

She'd spun around, intending to enlighten the fan on her view of the situation, but so many people clogged the area behind her she couldn't pick out the speaker.

She'd stalked to the car, knowing she could make at least one person listen to her.

And she would. As soon as he got home.

She eyed the heavy canvas backpack in the corner of the kitchen, the reason she wasn't worried for Bryan's safety. The backpack provided evidence he'd stopped by the house while she was at the game. And left again.

She didn't stop pacing until she caught the gleam of headlights through the blinds of the front window and heard a car pull up in the driveway.

She positioned herself in the kitchen near the refrigerator, Bryan's habitual first stop when he arrived home. She heard the key in the lock, then his footfalls as he approached. He didn't seem surprised to see her waiting for him.

"Hey, Keri. How's it going?" He spoke casually, as though it was a normal day and he'd just returned from school or basketball practice.

She wasn't wearing shoes, making the height difference between them even more substantial. She stabbed a finger in the direction of one of the kitchen chairs, not about to concede any advantage to her minor child. "Sit."

"What?"

"Just sit and listen," she said.

He sat but she remained standing. Thankfully Rose wasn't yet home, so Keri could speak freely. This was between her and Bryan. He regarded her with Maddy's eyes, making her more determined to set things right.

"I have never been as disappointed in you as I am right now," she said. "I know Becky wrote your paper, that Mr. Patterson changes your grades."

Bryan started to speak, but she cut him off. "No more denials. I want to hear why you have so little respect for yourself and your talent that you accept favors. I want to know why you're not doing your own schoolwork."

He said nothing, staring down at the hands he used to palm a basketball but not to do his own homework. Bella the cat slunk into the room, rubbing against Bryan's leg and taking up residence under the table, as though she sensed she was needed. Finally Bryan lifted his head, wet his lips and said, "Because I'm no good at school."

"What! Where'd you get that idea?"

His eyes darted away from hers. "Come on, Keri. Everybody knows the only thing I'm good at is basketball."

She gaped at him, feeling as though she was seeing him for the first time. Had she really been so caught up in Rose's problems she hadn't noticed Bryan had troubles of his own?

"That's not true," Keri said. "What about those photographs all over your room? They're fantastic."

"You think so?"

She saw with dismay that he didn't.

"Of course I do. And I'll tell you something else. More than one of your teachers has told me how smart you are."

Bryan shifted in his seat and said in a voice almost too soft to hear, "I hear my father was smart, too. And look what happened to him."

She pulled out one of the kitchen chairs and sat down next to him. "What does this have to do with your father?"

"Nothing." He rubbed a hand absently through his short hair. "Everything."

She said nothing, waiting for him to continue. The only sounds in the house were the hum of the refrigerator and soft whir of the heater. After a few moments, he said, "It's just that I want to be somebody. To make up for what he did."

She reached across the table and took one of his hands, hoping he felt the love flow from her. "You're not responsible for your father's mistakes."

"How can you be so sure I won't end up like him?" His grip tightened, as though he was holding on to her.

"Because I am." She gave his hand a light squeeze. "You're good and kind and smart and talented."

"I'm talented at basketball," he said, removing his hand and breaking the connection between them. "That's my best chance to make something of myself. But because of Coach Quinlan, I might not get the chance."

"Can't you tell he's trying to help you?" Keri asked. "Why do you think he's been so hard on you?"

Bryan didn't hesitate before answering, "Because he's a hard-ass."

"Because you remind him of himself. He used to be a hotshot basketball player, too, before he blew out his knee. Did you know that?"

Bryan looked very young when he replied, "I know he's trying to take basketball away from me."

"He's looking out for your best interests because he knows injuries end careers. And how do you repay him?" She couldn't stop the disappointment from seeping into her voice. "By going to the newspaper about what happened at Carolina State."

"I didn't do that," he said, but he was staring down at his hands when he issued the denial.

"But you know who did," she guessed.

"Hubie," he said. His partner in crime. "He knows somebody who used to play at Carolina State. I tried to talk him out of going to the paper, but he was pretty mad when Coach suspended me."

"Why did you try to talk him out of it?"

"Because it's a bogus charge," Bryan said. "Coach is too by-the-book to ever do something like that."

Yet Keri hadn't questioned the truth of the charges, at least not initially. "People believe what they read," she said, which was no excuse. "Some of the fans were saying terrible things about him at the game."

"They wanted us to win," Bryan said.

"You know that Springhill lost?"

He nodded. Of course he did, she thought. He had a cell phone and friends who stayed connected.

"Do you also know how much worse you made things for Grady by not showing up at the game?" she asked.

"I did show up. But when I got there, everybody was gone." He took a breath so ragged it seemed to hurt his chest. "I'm sorry about Coach Quinlan. I know you and Rose like him. I don't, but I never meant for him to resign."

"Resign? Who said anything about Grady resigning?"

"Hubie. He said Coach apologized to the team after

the game. And Garrett heard him tell Mr. Marco they needed to talk."

Keri got up so fast, she bumped her knee on the underside of the table. Bella meowed a protest. Ignoring the cat, she hurried to the closet to grab her coat and shove her feet into a pair of shoes she found there.

Bryan trailed her. "Where are you going?"

The answer, she thought, should have been obvious.

"To stop him," she said.

CHAPTER FIFTEEN

WILL SCHNEIDER'S NOTEBOOK made a soft thunking sound when he shut it, an action Grady viewed as symbolic. The reporter seemed to be closing the book on a chapter of Grady's life.

"I've got all I need," Schneider said in his typical staccato way of speaking. He rose from the oversize plaid sofa in Tony's family room, then stuck out a hand, shaking first Grady's hand, then Tony's.

"Thanks for coming," Grady said.

"Hey, you're doing me the favor." Schneider projected impatience to get going. "I'm the one who'll have the exclusive in tomorrow's paper."

Schneider would also write about Springhill being defeated in the first round of the regional basketball tournament, a loss Grady blamed on himself. After the game he'd looked into the disappointed faces of his players, grasped how much losing the game hurt and faced a tough truth: he hadn't given his team the best chance to win.

"Good luck, Coach," Schneider said. He raised a hand when Tony started to follow him to the front door. "It'll be quicker if I let myself out. Every minute counts when you're on deadline."

"Sure," Tony said, then called to Grady that he'd be right back. He returned a few moments later, carrying two long-necked bottles of beer. He tossed one to Grady. "How do you feel?"

"Like I did the right thing." Grady popped the cap on the beer, reluctant to elaborate. He'd talked enough basketball for one night. "You never did tell me where Mary Lynn went."

"The grocery store." Tony took a seat on the sofa next to Grady, settled back against the cushions and propped his feet on the coffee table. "She said she had a few things to pick up."

Grady raised an eyebrow at the dubious inflection in Tony's voice. "You don't believe she went to the store?"

"Yeah, I do." Tony sighed heavily. "But to get out of the house, not because we need groceries."

"Things aren't any better?"

"They're worse," Tony said, briefly closing his eyes. "How about you? How are things with you and my ex?"

The verbal barbs Keri had shot at him still stung, but not as much as the pain of losing her. "Not good," Grady said. "But I still don't like you referring to Keri as *your* anything."

"Noted." Tony took a long swallow of his beer, an action that Grady mirrored. They sat in silence for a while before Tony remarked, "We're some pair, aren't we?"

THE RED MIATA BACKING FAR too quickly out of Tony and Mary Lynn Marco's driveway looked familiar to Keri. She pulled to the curb in back of Grady's Toyota and cut her car's engine, craning her neck to get a look at the driver.

The glow from a nearby streetlight briefly touched upon the unmistakable features of Will Schneider.

"Oh, no," she said aloud.

She was too late. Grady hadn't only offered Tony his resignation, he'd invited the press to witness the show.

The Miata reached the street, its tires squealing after Will put the car in Drive and sped off. With a sense of helplessness, Keri watched the Miata's taillights grow smaller. Her hands still gripping the steering wheel, she considered following Will back to the newspaper office.

But what good would that do? She'd never be able to talk a newshound like Will out of printing the story.

She got out of her car and hurried toward the house, nearly reaching the entrance before the garage door slid open. Keri stopped moving, watching as Mary Lynn maneuvered a blue compact car as cute as she was into the double-car garage. Mary Lynn got out of the car, slamming the door behind her. She stalked toward Keri, outrage evident in her every step.

"You've got a hell of a lot of nerve," she said, her voice cutting through the quiet night, her warm breath visible in the chilly air.

Keri blinked. "Excuse me?"

"You heard me." Mary Lynn glared up at Keri, the three-quarters moon plus the porch light enabling Keri to see that her blue eyes were huge in her pale face. "What did you do? Peek in the garage to make sure my car wasn't there?"

"No, I—"

"Did Tony tell you we're having problems? Is that why you're here?"

"I don't—"

"Because you can just turn around and go home. I don't care if you used to be engaged to Tony, he's my husband. And you can't have him."

Her tirade over, she glowered fiercely at Keri, as though she might tackle her if she tried to gain entrance to the house.

"I'm not here because of Tony." Keri gestured to the dark street, where Grady's car was parked in front of hers. "I came to see Grady."

A furrow appeared between Mary Lynn's finely shaped brows. "Why?"

"Because he just resigned and I mean to talk him out of it," Keri said, then realized that hadn't been what Mary Lynn was asking. She drew in a deep breath. "And because I'm in love with him."

"But I thought…" Mary Lynn's voice faltered, then rallied. "I thought you still loved Tony."

Keri shook her head. "Tony's a good guy, but I don't think I ever truly loved him. Not the way I love Grady."

Mary Lynn pressed her lips together, seeming to digest the information. Then she sniffed, looking utterly miserable. "Then what Tony feels must be one-sided."

"Not unless you don't love him back." Keri put a hand on the sleeve of the other woman's red coat, encouraged when Mary Lynn didn't shrug off her touch. "Because Tony told me he's crazy in love with you."

A mixture of hope and disbelief appeared on Mary Lynn's face, with disbelief winning. "But I saw you with Tony in front of the newspaper office today."

Had that really been today? It seemed as though it

had been much longer since Keri and Tony had resolved their past.

"I stopped by the high school and saw him follow you to the parking lot," Mary Lynn continued in a strangled voice. "When he got in his car to follow you, I followed him."

Keri tried to remember what happened while she talked to Tony that could have upset Mary Lynn. "You saw me lean into the car and kiss him," she guessed.

Mary Lynn nodded, her enormous eyes filled with a wealth of sadness.

"Listen to me. There was nothing romantic about that kiss. Tony just apologized for abandoning me when I took in Rose and Bryan. It was a kiss of forgiveness, Mary Lynn. That's what Tony wanted from me all along."

"Really?" Mary Lynn asked, her voice spiking with hope. In the next instant, her lower lip trembled. "Why should I believe you?"

Keri tried to put herself in Mary Lynn's position, silently acknowledging how difficult it could be to see through the misdirection to the truth.

"If I've learned anything these past few months," she told Mary Lynn, "it's that things aren't always what they seem."

Mary Lynn appeared to consider that. Soon, a tremulous smile bent the corners of her mouth. She nodded toward the open garage, through which Keri spotted a side door that led into the house.

"Come inside," Mary Lynn said. "I've got to set things right with my man and you've got to talk yours out of making a big mistake."

THE SOUND OF A DOOR OPENING caused Grady to take another pull of beer. The sooner he finished the brew, the sooner he could leave Tony and Mary Lynn alone, hopefully to work out their problems.

"That'll be Mary Lynn." Tony got up from the sofa, took a few steps toward the kitchen and stopped dead. "And Keri."

Keri? Grady twisted his body and craned his neck. Sure enough, Keri walked into the family room alongside Mary Lynn. Her brown hair, usually brushed so neatly, was tousled. Her color was high, her eyes bright, the set of her mouth determined.

"I'm sorry to barge in like this," Keri said, addressing Tony.

"You don't have to apologize, Keri," Mary Lynn said, clutching at her arm supportively, as though the two of them were…friends? "Just tell Grady what you have to say."

"You came here to see me?" Grady asked, half rising. "Why?"

"Go ahead, Keri," Mary Lynn encouraged. "Tell him."

Keri slanted Mary Lynn what Grady interpreted as a grateful look, then walked past Tony deeper into the family room. Grady watched Keri's graceful approach, but his peripheral vision caught Mary Lynn grabbing Tony's hand and tugging him out of the room.

Keri didn't stop until she was in front of the sofa. Grady sat back down, and Keri positioned herself on the edge of the maple coffee table across from him.

"You can't leave Springhill basketball now, Grady." Keri leaned forward and captured his hands, imparting warmth where he hadn't been aware it was lacking. "Those kids might not know it, but they need you. They didn't win tonight, but so what? It's more important they become good people than good basketball players. You can make that happen."

"Thanks," he said, touched by the praise. "But I don't know what you're talking about. I'm not going anywhere."

"You didn't just resign?"

"Hell, no," he said.

"But…" She released his hands. "But I saw Will Schneider leaving. If you didn't resign, why was he here?"

"I gave him my side of what happened at Carolina State," Grady said.

"You told him about the false accusations?"

He stared into her eyes, which looked back, clear and trusting. "You know I was set up as the fall guy?"

Her expression drew into a pained look. "Not at first, I didn't. And I'm sorry about that, Grady. I should have been able to look beneath the surface to the man you really are."

"I shouldn't have let my stupid pride get in the way of telling you," he said. "Actually, I should have told everybody. Especially after Schneider ran that story. For the record, I never knew about the secret fund and I didn't give recruits a dime. Bud Hardgrove shifted the blame to me so the NCAA would go easy on the program and he wouldn't get fired."

"Why did you decide to tell?" Keri asked.

"Because we might have won tonight if I had," he stated, the knowledge as grating as when he'd reached the conclusion.

"How do you figure that?"

"My players. It's hard enough being in the regionals without your best player. It's harder when everybody's coming down on your coach."

Her mouth gaped, the little space between her front teeth visible. "You can't think you were the reason the team lost."

"Maybe not," he said. "But the distraction sure didn't help."

"Is that why you apologized to your players?"

"Yeah," he said, "but how'd you hear about that?"

"Hubie told Bryan."

"I didn't apologize for suspending Bryan," Grady said, feeling his muscles knot. Every other time he and Keri had talked about Bryan, the discussion had deteriorated. "I still believe it was the right thing to do."

"I know it was," Keri said. "I was so blind, Grady. I know now that all the things you said about Bryan are true."

Grady didn't ask how she'd arrived at that conclusion. All that mattered was for Keri to take the steps that would set Bryan on the right path.

"Oh, Grady." She blinked a few times, her eyes tellingly wet. "I was so involved with Rose's problems I didn't pay enough attention to what was going on with Bryan. I've been a terrible mom."

He touched her cheek, wiping away the slight dampness under her eyes. "That's crazy. You're doing an incredible job. Rose is terrific. Bryan's a little misguided, but he's a great kid, too. Just like you keep telling me."

"But—"

He put a finger over her mouth to silence her. "No buts.

You took in those kids when they had nobody else. When you were hardly older than a child yourself."

"Anybody would have done it."

"Very few people would have done it," he countered. "And that's only one of the reasons I'm in love with you."

Wonder replaced the guilt in her eyes. "You love me?"

"Oh, yeah," he said, quite sure he'd used the correct term for the emotion that seemed to be pulsing through his very veins. "I love everything about you. Even the way you leap to Bryan's defense."

"Really?" she asked, looking as though she wasn't sure whether to believe him.

"Yes. In fact, I'm so crazy in love with you my heart is racing." He laid her hand over his heart to prove the truth of his words. "Part love. Part fear."

"What are you afraid of?"

He wet his lips, cleared his throat and put his heart on the line. "That you don't love me back."

"Silly man." Her face split into a beautiful smile, erasing any lingering trace of guilt or doubt. "Of course I love you back."

She laid her hands on both sides of his face and kissed him with her soft, warm, wonderful lips. And just like that, the shadow that had hung over Grady for the better part of two years disappeared. As if it had never been.

EPILOGUE

Three months later

THE SUN SHONE DOWN ON the outdoor track outside Spring-hill High where eight girls approached the blocks for the four-hundred meter dash, illuminating a nearly perfect day in mid-May.

Even though the competitors wore different numbers on their chests and the varying colors of the schools they represented, from a distance all but one looked remarkably alike in their skimpy track uniforms.

The exception wore her long golden-brown hair tied back in a ponytail, the black-and-gold colors of Spring-hill and a specially designed prosthetic leg.

Keri leapt to her feet, curled her lips over her teeth, put her thumb and index finger in her mouth and whistled the way her brother taught her when they were kids. "Go, Rosie!"

Beside her, Grady let out a hearty laugh. "The race hasn't started yet, Keri."

"You tell me that at every meet."

"And every time you say you can't help yourself."

"I can't," Keri agreed happily.

On the track, the contestants approached their blocks. Tony Marco, standing alongside the chain-rail fence alongside his wife, Mary Lynn, turned around and gave them a thumbs-up. Mary Lynn grinned and waved.

The only person doing any running yet was Bryan, who sprinted into view dressed in gym shorts and a T-shirt. His school backpack and the camera he usually carried with him bounced against his back as he bounded up the bleachers to join them.

Bryan was sweating lightly, courtesy of the open gym sessions Grady made available for his players in the off season. Grady had peeled away from the gym ten minutes ago, leaving his assistant coach to supervise.

"You're just in time," Keri told Bryan an instant before the crack of the starter's gun sounded and the runners took off en masse.

Bryan cupped his hands around his mouth and shouted, "Go, Rosie, go!"

Keri and Bryan were already standing. Grady got to his feet, occupying the space between them so they stood three abreast.

Rose pumped her arms, striding so effortlessly around the track it seemed as though she was gliding. The competitors ran around the first curve, with Rose solidly in the middle of the group. Keri's throat swelled with so much pride she was momentarily speechless.

By the second curve, Rose was running neck-and-neck with one of the other competitors. Keri peeked through the fingers she'd placed over her eyes, both afraid to watch and to miss a single second of the race.

"Hold her off, Rosie!" Bryan bellowed.

Rose and her opponent matched each other stride for stride, with Rose maintaining the slimmest of leads.

"You can do it, Zoom Zoom!" Grady shouted.

As if propelled by her cheering section, Rose seemed to run faster, gaining a precious step on her rival.

"C'mon, c'mon, c'mon," added Keri, the only thing Keri seemed capable of saying as the two girls approached the finish line.

Rose planted on her flesh-and-blood leg, then extended her prosthesis to cross the tape solidly in seventh place.

"All right!" Bryan and Grady shouted in unison, turning to slap each other's palms.

"She did it! She did it!" Keri threw her arms around Grady's neck and gave him a short but enthusiastic kiss.

Rose looked up toward her cheering section, grinned broadly and blew them a kiss.

"It doesn't get any better than that," Keri said, still holding on to Grady.

"Maybe not. But I've got something pretty cool to show you, too." Bryan eagerly moved aside his camera, reached into his backpack and pulled out a paper filled with equations. He held it out to them proudly. Atop it in bold red pen was a B.

"That's wonderful, Bryan," Keri said. "I knew you could do it."

"Jackie's a great algebra tutor," Bryan stated. "Now, if only I could get her to be my girlfriend."

"She's still resisting you, huh?" Grady asked.

"Yeah, but I'm working on it." Bryan shifted his weight from one foot to the other. "I was thinking of asking you for some tips."

"Me?" Grady asked in surprise. In the months Keri and Grady had been dating, Bryan had been respectful but not overly friendly. His only in-depth discussion with Grady had come after the news broke that the Carolina State basketball program was in trouble again and that Bud Hardgrove had been fired.

"Sure," Bryan said. "You must have worked some kind of mojo on Keri."

Grady threw his head back and laughed. Bryan joined in, giving Keri hope that Grady's "mojo" was starting to work on Bryan, too.

The three of them descended the bleachers in tandem, pausing to celebrate Rose's accomplishment with the Marcos before going to the fence to congratulate a blushing Rose.

"I can't believe what a big deal you guys are making," she said with an eye roll. "It was only the first time I didn't come in last."

"Haven't you been listening to me, Zoom Zoom?" Grady said. "The triumph isn't in winning. It's in competing. And you competed the heck out of that race."

After Rose jogged off to rejoin her teammates, Keri anchored her hands on Grady's shoulders and stood on tiptoes to kiss him without an ounce of self-consciousness.

"Why'd you do that?" Grady asked when she broke off the kiss, the sun reflected in his hazel eyes.

She could have given him a dozen answers. For teaching Rose to use her prosthesis. For helping Keri see that Bryan was heading for trouble. For being the right kind of man. But one response summed up all of the others perfectly.

"Because," she said simply, "I love you."

* * * * *

THOROUGHBRED LEGACY
The stakes are high when it comes to love,
horse racing, family secrets
and broken promises.

A new exciting
Harlequin continuity series
coming soon!
Led by New York Times *bestselling author*
Elizabeth Bevarly
FLIRTING WITH TROUBLE

Here's a preview!

THE DOOR CLOSED behind them, throwing them into darkness and leaving them utterly alone. And the next thing Daniel knew, he heard himself saying, "Marnie, I'm sorry about the way things turned out in Del Mar."

She said nothing at first, only strode across the room and stared out the window beside him. Although he couldn't see her well in the darkness—he still hadn't switched on a light…but then, neither had she—he imagined her expression was a little preoccupied, a little anxious, a little confused.

Finally, very softly, she said, "Are you?"

He nodded, then, worried she wouldn't be able to see the gesture, added, "Yeah. I am. I should have said goodbye to you."

"Yes, you should have."

Actually, he thought, there were a lot of things he should have done in Del Mar. He'd had *a lot* riding on the Pacific Classic, and even more on his entry, Little Joe, but after meeting Marnie, the Pacific Classic had been the last thing on Daniel's mind. His loss at Del Mar had pretty much ended his career before it had even begun, and he'd had to start all over again, rebuilding from nothing.

He simply had not then and did not now have room in

his life for a woman as potent as Marnie Roberts. He was a horseman first and foremost. From the time he was a schoolboy, he'd known what he wanted to do with his life—be the best possible trainer he could be.

He had to make sure Marnie understood—and he understood, too—why things had ended the way they had eight years ago. He just wished he could find the words to do that. Hell, he wished he could find the *thoughts* to do that.

"You made me forget things, Marnie, things that I really needed to remember. And that scared the hell out of me. Little Joe should have won the Classic. He was by far the best horse entered in that race. But I didn't give him the attention he needed and deserved that week, because all I could think about was you. Hell, when I woke up that morning all I wanted to do was lie there and look at you, and then wake you up and make love to you again. If I hadn't left when I did—the way I did—I might still be lying there in that bed with you, thinking about nothing else."

"And would that be so terrible?" she asked.

"Of course not," he told her. "But that wasn't why I was in Del Mar," he repeated. "I was in Del Mar to win a race. That was my job. And my work was the most important thing to me."

She said nothing for a moment, only studied his face in the darkness as if looking for the answer to a very important question. Finally she asked, "And what's the most important thing to you now, Daniel?"

Wasn't the answer to that obvious? "My work," he answered automatically.

She nodded slowly. "Of course," she said softly. "That is, after all, what you do best."

Her comment, too, puzzled him. She made it sound as if being good at what he did was a bad thing.

She bit her lip thoughtfully, her eyes fixed on his, glimmering in the scant moonlight that was filtering through the window. And damned if Daniel didn't find himself wanting to pull her into his arms and kiss her. But as much as it might have felt as if no time had passed since Del Mar, there were eight years between now and then. And eight years was a long time in the best of circumstances. For Daniel and Marnie, it was virtually a lifetime.

So Daniel turned and started for the door, then halted. He couldn't just walk away and leave things as they were, unsettled. He'd done that eight years ago and regretted it.

"It *was* good to see you again, Marnie," he said softly. And since he was being honest, he added, "I hope we see each other again."

She didn't say anything in response, only stood silhouetted against the window with her arms wrapped around her in a way that made him wonder whether she was doing it because she was cold, or if she just needed something—someone—to hold on to. In either case, Daniel understood. There was an emptiness clinging to him that he suspected would be there for a long time.

* * * * *

THOROUGHBRED LEGACY
coming soon wherever books are sold!

Thoroughbred *Legacy*

Launching in June 2008

A dramatic new 12-book continuity that embodies the American Dream.

Meet the Prestons, owners of Quest Stables, a successful horse-racing and breeding empire. But the lives, loves and reputations of this hardworking family are put at risk when a breeding scandal unfolds.

Flirting with Trouble

by *New York Times* bestselling author

ELIZABETH BEVARLY

Eight years ago, publicist Marnie Roberts spent seven days of bliss with Australian horse trainer Daniel Whittleson. But just as quickly, he disappeared. Now Marnie is heading to Australia to finally confront the man she's never been able to forget.

The stakes are high when it comes to love, horse racing, family secrets and broken promises.

A new exciting Harlequin continuity series coming soon!

www.eHarlequin.com

HT38984R

Cole's Red-Hot Pursuit

Cole Westmoreland is a man who gets what he
wants. And he wants independent and sultry
Patrina Forman! She resists him—until a Montana
blizzard traps them together. For three delicious
nights, Cole indulges Patrina with his brand of
seduction. When the sun comes out, Cole and
Patrina are left to wonder—will this be the end of
the passion that storms between them?

Look for

COLE'S RED-HOT
PURSUIT

by USA TODAY bestselling author

BRENDA
JACKSON

Available in June 2008 wherever you buy books.

Always Powerful, Passionate and Provocative.

REQUEST YOUR FREE BOOKS!

2 FREE NOVELS PLUS 2 FREE GIFTS!

HARLEQUIN®

Super Romance®

Exciting, emotional, unexpected!

YES! Please send me 2 FREE Harlequin Superromance® novels and my 2 FREE gifts (gifts are worth about $10). After receiving them, if I don't wish to receive any more books, I can return the shipping statement marked "cancel." If I don't cancel, I will receive 6 brand-new novels every month and be billed just $4.69 per book in the U.S. or $5.24 per book in Canada, plus 25¢ shipping and handling per book and applicable taxes, if any*. That's a savings of close to 15% off the cover price! I understand that accepting the 2 free books and gifts places me under no obligation to buy anything. I can always return a shipment and cancel at any time. Even if I never buy another book from Harlequin, the two free books and gifts are mine to keep forever.

135 HDN EEX7   336 HDN EEYK

Name	(PLEASE PRINT)	
Address		Apt. #
City	State/Prov.	Zip/Postal Code

Signature (if under 18, a parent or guardian must sign)

Mail to the **Harlequin Reader Service:**
IN U.S.A.: P.O. Box 1867, Buffalo, NY 14240-1867
IN CANADA: P.O. Box 609, Fort Erie, Ontario L2A 5X3

Not valid to current subscribers of Harlequin Superromance books.

Want to try two free books from another line?
Call 1-800-873-8635 or visit www.morefreebooks.com.

* Terms and prices subject to change without notice. N.Y. residents add applicable sales tax. Canadian residents will be charged applicable provincial taxes and GST. This offer is limited to one order per household. All orders subject to approval. Credit or debit balances in a customer's account(s) may be offset by any other outstanding balance owed by or to the customer. Please allow 4 to 6 weeks for delivery. Offer available while quantities last.

Your Privacy: Harlequin is committed to protecting your privacy. Our Privacy Policy is available online at www.eHarlequin.com or upon request from the Reader Service. From time to time we make our lists of customers available to reputable third parties who may have a product or service of interest to you. If you would prefer we not share your name and address, please check here. ☐

HSR08

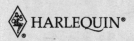

HARLEQUIN®

American ★ Romance®

DOUBLE THE REASONS
TO PARTY!

**We are celebrating American Romance's
25th Anniversary just in time to make
your Fourth of July celebrations
sensational with Kraft!**

American Romance is presenting
four fabulous recipes from Kraft,
to make sure your Fourth of July
celebrations are a hit! Each
American Romance book in June contains a different
recipe—a salad, appetizer, main course or a dessert.
Collect all four in June wherever books are sold!

kraftfoods.com—
deliciously simple. everyday.

Or visit kraftcanada.com
for more delicious meal ideas.

www.eHarlequin.com   KRAFTBPA

COMING NEXT MONTH

#1494 HER REASON TO STAY • Anna Adams
Twins

Coming to Honesty, Virginia, is Daphne Soder's chance to forge a family with her newfound twin. First she must face her sister's protective lawyer, Patrick Gannon. Their confrontations ignite sparks she never expected, giving her a different reason to stay.

#1495 FALLING FOR THE DEPUTY • Amy Frazier

The more Chloe Atherton pushes, the more Deputy Sheriff Mack Whittaker pulls away. However, keen to prove herself, she'll stop at nothing to get a good story for her newspaper—even if it means digging up the traumatic episode in his past. But can she risk hurting this quiet, compassionate man? A man she's beginning to care too much about...

#1496 NOT WITHOUT HER FAMILY • Beth Andrews
Count on a Cop

It's nothing but trouble for Jack Martin, chief of police, when Kelsey Reagan blows into town. Her ex-con brother is the prime suspect in a murder, and Kelsey vows to prove he's innocent. And now Jack's young daughter is falling for Kelsey…just like her dad.

#1497 TO PROTECT THE CHILD • Anna DeStefano
Atlanta Heroes

Waking in the hospital with no memory leaves FBI operative Alexa Vega doubting who she can trust. Except for Dr. Robert Livingston, that is. In his care, she recovers enough to risk going back to finish what she started—saving a child in danger. But if she survives the FBI sting, will Alexa find the strength to truly trust in Robert's love?

#1498 A SOLDIER COMES HOME • Cindi Myers
Single Father

Captain Ray Hughes never expected to return from active duty to an empty house and the role of single father. Thankfully his neighbor Chrissie Evans lends a hand. Soon his feelings toward her are more than neighborly. But can he take a chance with love again?

#1499 ALWAYS A MOTHER • Linda Warren
Everlasting Love

Once upon a time, Claire Rennels made a decision that changed her life forever. She kept the baby, married the man she loved and put her dreams of college on hold. Now her kids are grown and she's pregnant again. Is she ready for another baby? And is love enough to keep her and Dean together after the sacrifices she's made?

HSRCNM0508